THE GIRL IN THE PAINTING

A Jefferson Tayte Genealogical Mystery

OTHER TITLES BY STEVE ROBINSON

The Penmaker's Wife
The Secret Wife

The Jefferson Tayte Series

In the Blood
To the Grave
The Last Queen of England
The Lost Empress
Kindred
Dying Games
Letters from the Dead

THE GIRL IN THE PAINTING

A Jefferson Tayte Genealogical Mystery

by
STEVE ROBINSON

Alchera

This is a work of fiction. Names, characters, organisations, places, events, and incidents are either products of the author's imagination or are used fictitiously. Any resemblance to actual persons, living or dead, or actual events is purely coincidental.

Text copyright © 2021 by Steve Robinson
All rights reserved.

No part of this book may be reproduced, or stored in a retrieval system, or transmitted in any form or by any means, electronic, mechanical, photocopying, recording, or otherwise, without express written permission of the publisher.

Published by Alchera, London

ISBN-13: 979-8595334068

For my wife, Karen

CONTENTS

PROLOGUE	1
CHAPTER ONE	4
CHAPTER TWO	18
CHAPTER THREE	24
CHAPTER FOUR	29
CHAPTER FIVE	34
CHAPTER SIX	41
CHAPTER SEVEN	50
CHAPTER EIGHT	55
CHAPTER NINE	63
CHAPTER TEN	69
CHAPTER ELEVEN	73
CHAPTER TWELVE	77
CHAPTER THIRTEEN	84
CHAPTER FOURTEEN	90
CHAPTER FIFTEEN	94
CHAPTER SIXTEEN	102
CHAPTER SEVENTEEN	110
CHAPTER EIGHTEEN	117

CHAPTER NINETEEN	124
CHAPTER TWENTY	130
CHAPTER TWENTY-ONE	135
CHAPTER TWENTY-TWO	142
CHAPTER TWENTY-THREE	147
CHAPTER TWENTY-FOUR	153
CHAPTER TWENTY-FIVE	158
CHAPTER TWENTY-SIX	163
CHAPTER TWENTY-SEVEN	169
CHAPTER TWENTY-EIGHT	176
CHAPTER TWENTY-NINE	182
ACKNOWLEDGEMENTS	189
ABOUT THE AUTHOR	191

PROLOGUE

North Kensington, London
1891

Jess had overheard people describing the enclave of Notting Dale as the West End Avernus several times before. Until recently, however, she'd had no idea what that meant. It was only when she began to hear those same people refer to the area as hell on earth that she twigged. She had to agree with them, too, but even so, she would stay if she could. Her home in the Potteries and Piggeries, for all its many cramped and unsanitary faults, was the only home she had known.

She had been born there one July day, twelve years ago to the month, perhaps to that very day for all she knew, because she had never been told the precise date of her birth. She had watched her younger siblings come into the world and cry their first breaths there, and she had watched some of them die there, lost to disease or neglect. She did not wish to leave, not yet at least, and certainly not like this, but despite her wishes, she feared she would soon have to.

'Mr Butterfill's coming for me,' she said, a baby cradled in each arm. 'I don't know who'll look after you then,' she added. 'After I'm gone, that is.' She continued to rock the twins back and forth to keep them quiet, as she'd been told to, as she was always told to whenever they cried, which was often. 'I don't know who'll take care of Charlie and Hannah, neither. Whatever am I to do?'

One of the twins began to blow bubbles at her. To their father's delight, they were both girls. He only ever wanted girls. To Harry Bates, a boy held comparatively little value. 'Nothing more than a gaping mouth to feed,' he'd said when little Charlie was born, and Jess imagined he'd said the same when her older brother, Thomas, was born, although Thomas was the lucky one as far as Jess was concerned. Working as a pure-finder, collecting dog faeces to sell to the tanners, Thomas hadn't been able to bring much into the house by way of money, so he'd been thrown out on his ear the day after his twelfth birthday and made to fend for himself. At least he was free to do as he pleased, Jess thought, free to make his own decisions about where he lived, for whom he would work, and whom he might someday marry. Little Charlie had already been promised to the sweep for a few bob when he was old enough, which, although he was still only six years old, would be soon.

'I have dreams, you know,' Jess told the twins, bouncing them a little now, aware that they were waking up. 'I want to work in a fancy factory someday, with regular hours, earning a proper wage so I can see to it that you're okay. How am I supposed do that now, with Mr Butterfill coming?'

One of the twins blinked, her eyes dark and shiny as coal in the low candlelight.

'We both know whose fault it is, don't we?' Jess said. She nodded at the baby, as if hearing her reply. 'That's right,' she whispered. 'It's Dad's fault, isn't it? He made this happen, didn't he? He didn't have to, but he did. He's the one what's to blame. He's the one who—'

She stopped mid-sentence and caught her breath as a distant but familiar sound reached her ears. She turned towards the window she was sitting by, in the downstairs front room. It wasn't quite dark out, but she could see very little through the yellowing net curtain and the grimy glass. She could, however, clearly hear the brass tip of a walking cane clicking on the narrow pavement outside. She knew the sound, and more importantly the fast-paced rhythm, well enough.

It was Mr Butterfill.

'Please keep walking,' she said under her breath, desperation in her tone as the sound grew louder, closer. 'Please, please keep walking.'

A moment later, the click of the cane stopped, and Jess's heart began to race. She swallowed the lump that had risen in her throat. Then she jumped in her seat, upsetting the twins as she heard the tip of Mr Butterfill's cane rapping ominously at the front door.

'He's here,' she told the twins. 'The old man what I told you about. He's come for me. Oh, Lord! Whatever am I to do?'

CHAPTER ONE

Present day

A car horn blasted behind him, and Jefferson Tayte began to swerve and snake in the road as he struggled to control both his briefcase, which he'd attached to a bungee cord around his shoulders, and the tiny wheels of the foldaway bicycle he was riding. He fought the urge to raise a fist at the impatient London cab driver as he passed, and instead stuck out his arm to make a turn, heading, as he did every Wednesday and Friday at around six in the evening, for the Marcus Brown School of Family History.

The school, teaching genealogy rather than practising it, was an entirely new venture for him, and a far cry from his old life in America before he'd moved to England. Evening classes had seemed the way to go, although he also ran a class on Saturday mornings for those who could only make the weekends. He knew people were often busy with their work at other times, so it made perfect sense. It was cheaper for him, too. It meant he could share the space he rented with someone else. He'd turned down a generous offer to fund something far grander, having decided that he wanted to make the move from professional genealogist to teacher alone, in case he wasn't any good at it and the venture failed. That way, if it did, he was only letting himself down.

He turned another corner and the low, early May sunshine suddenly blinded him. It made him sweat all the more as he made his way along the street, taking in the regimented facade of the King's College London Waterloo Campus as he passed. The sight of it always made him think how appropriate it had been to position his school of genealogy so close to such a prestigious seat of learning.

By the time Tayte came in sight of his own humble seat of learning, just a few minutes later, he was panting harder than any forty-something would care to admit. He was thankful, however, that this leg of his journey from the Docklands area where he lived was almost over, even though he'd only ridden his bicycle the relatively short distance to and from the Tube station at either end.

The school was on a narrow, quiet little street that was in full shade, for which Tayte was also thankful. He pulled up beside an iron bollard outside a three-storey red-brick building, brakes squealing and juddering under his weight as he came to a stop. Dismounting, he quickly folded the bicycle away, always a little impressed with himself these days at how adept he had become at doing so.

When he'd first received the bicycle, for a good many months it would take him forever to pack it down. He'd often given up altogether. Now, he considered himself a pro, worthy of a merchandise marketing video. The bicycle had been a birthday present, almost a year ago now, something to help keep him active and burn a few calories. No one had said as much at the time, but he was under no illusion that it had been given to him for any other reason. He was all for being 'green', but he knew the gift was intended to help save himself, not the planet.

Tayte took off his helmet, clipped the strap around the bicycle's frame, and tucked it all up under his arm before striding over to the entrance of the building. He paused, as he always did, to take in the brass nameplate he'd had made, bearing the name of his old friend and mentor, just to remind himself that he really was a teacher now, as Marcus Brown had been.

He laughed to himself. 'If you could see me now, Marcus, old friend,' he told the nameplate. Then before he went inside he gazed up at the heavens, wondering whether Marcus could.

The second-floor room Tayte had rented was used for art classes during the day. He had a locked cupboard all to himself, as did the art master, whose easels were stacked against the wall inside the door to his left. His own classes didn't begin for another hour, but he liked to arrive early, to prepare for the lesson, and to set up the folding chairs and desks he'd bought, which were stacked against the wall to his right. Directly ahead of him, before the only windows in the room, was a tired oak desk that had been there when he moved in, which he and the art master shared.

He strode up to it and tucked his bicycle out of sight behind it, then he swung his tan leather briefcase around in front of him, unclipped it from the bungee cord and set it down on the desk, wondering how many people would turn up for class this evening. There were usually five or six on a good day. It was an inauspicious start, perhaps, but at least it was a start, and the intimate nature of the classes suited him while he was still finding his feet. He imagined his students, who so far ranged in age anywhere from seventeen to seventy, did as well.

Tayte went over to his cupboard and unlocked it, took out a towel and wiped the sweat off his brow. Then he forced a comb through his thick black hair, which was more untidy than usual on account of his bicycle helmet. There was a tall mirror inside the door, which quickly told him that the comb was fighting a losing battle, and that his crumpled tan linen suit was a bad choice for a bicycle ride on a warm evening, but what could he do? He wasn't about to compromise on his preferred choice of suit just because he'd become a teacher, and he figured his hair would settle down by the time the class began.

He went back to his desk and took out a pile of papers from his briefcase, ready to pass them around when his students arrived. During the past month he'd been running a series of lessons on the British Isles, and this week it was all about finding your Irish ancestors – a subject that had been close to many of his American clients' hearts when he was living and working in Washington, DC. He picked up one of the handouts and checked it over to ensure he'd included the homework assignment at the back. Then he set up all the chairs and desks in neat rows, knowing he'd need less than half of them.

With everything in place and twenty minutes to spare, Tayte sat back in the chair at his desk and set his briefcase down beside him. He pulled out his sandwiches, which were lettuce and tomato as usual, and a few Hershey's Miniatures. He knew the chocolates kind of missed the point of the low-calorie sandwiches, but he figured one step at a time was the way to go. He didn't want to shock his system too hard. He took a bite of the sandwich, pulled the same dour face he always did, and quickly popped one of the chocolates into his mouth to help it down.

Then he waited.

◆ ◆ ◆

Tayte's introductory class on tracing Irish ancestry lasted an hour and a half. During that time, while everyone followed the lesson on their laptops, he spoke about the importance of Irish civil records and tax surveys, and of church registers and census reports, being the four main resources available to family historians searching Irish records online. He'd immediately gone on to inform his students to be mindful of the fact that many records were destroyed during the Irish Civil War of 1922-3, including a great number of early Irish census documents. He spoke enthusiastically to an attentive audience of just five budding genealogists, currently all female, four having been regulars at his Wednesday class for several weeks now. The fifth, however – a young woman in her twenties, by Tayte's estimation – was entirely new, which he liked to see.

From little acorns, he reminded himself as the class ended and everyone stood up to leave. 'I'll see you next time,' he said with a wave and a smile. 'And wherever your research takes you, remember the first rule of genealogy.'

'We know,' one of them replied, as if they had all heard the answer a thousand times before. It was Betty Atcherley, a white-haired woman with the kindest of faces. She was the eldest of the group and Tayte's first student. She looked around at everyone, smiling, as she often did. 'What is it, ladies?' she asked them.

A moment later, everyone chanted, 'Talk to the family!'

Everyone, that is, except one. It was the newcomer.

As the class filtered out of the room, quietly chatting about the lesson while Tayte packed his things back into his briefcase, the young woman slowly approached his desk. She stopped six feet away, as if perhaps shy of him, or nervous for some reason, and just stood there, saying nothing.

Tayte looked up. 'Natalie, isn't it?' he said, offering her a smile. 'Natalie Cooper.'

'Nat,' she said. 'Everyone calls me Nat.'

She wore a thick, bright-blue jumper, the sleeves of which hung down over her hands, a red woollen skirt that came to her knees, and opaque lime-green tights. Tayte studied her petite frame momentarily, his eyes wandering down to her heavy-looking purple Doc Martens, thinking that the colours of her clothing were as random and colourful as the many highlights in her otherwise black hair.

'Well then, Nat,' he said, noticing that she had an orange folder under her arm, adding to the rainbow. 'What is it I can do for you? Did you enjoy the class? Enough to come again?'

Nat gave a firm nod, flicking her tongue at the stud in her lower lip. She pulled the folder out from under her arm. 'There's something in here I'd like to show you,' she said. 'If you have a moment.'

Tayte was intrigued. 'Of course,' he said. 'What is it?'

Nat took her folder to the desk and opened it, suddenly having found a spring in her step. 'I've been working on my family tree and I'm stuck. I was hoping you could help get my research moving again.'

'A brick wall, eh?' Tayte said, gazing over the contents of the folder as Nat spread everything out. 'Let's take a look at what you have.'

There wasn't much.

'It's not about Irish ancestry,' Nat said, sounding apologetic. 'At least, I don't think it is.'

'That's okay,' Tayte said, eyeing a Polaroid photograph of a painting that was attached to the topmost file with a paperclip. 'What exactly is the problem?'

'You're looking at it,' Nat said. 'I believe the girl in that photo is one of my great-great-grandfather's sisters. I know from the 1891 census that she was born in 1879, and where she lived at the time the census was taken, of course, but I can't find anything else about her. It's as if she just vanished.'

Tayte raised his eyebrows. 'I see,' he said, already beginning to feel the sense of intrigue that he had to admit he'd missed more than a little since he'd hung up his metaphorical hat and started teaching. 'Genealogical brick walls can often seem like that,' he added, 'but there's usually an explanation out there somewhere. The trick is knowing how to find it.'

'Do you think you could help me to find it?' Nat asked, her eyes widening. 'To break down this particular brick wall?'

Tayte couldn't help but notice a sense of desperation as she spoke. It was written in the lines on her face and the tone of her voice. It made him wonder whether there was more riding on his answer than he as yet knew. 'Well, let's see what else you have here,' he said, looking at her records again.

Nat pushed a bright pink ribbon of hair back over one ear and leaned in. She pulled out one of the records. 'This is from the 1891 census I mentioned. Here's my great-great-grandfather, Charlie Bates, who was five at the time. His father was Harry Bates, the head of the household.' She pointed to the names on the record as she spoke, highlighting each in turn. 'His wife, Gertrude, and their four other children, Jessie, the eldest, Hannah, and twin girls, Emma and Lillian, who were just babies.' She handed the record to Tayte and foraged for another. 'I found these Barnardo's orphanage records showing that Charlie and Hannah were, for some reason, at the same home for orphans by 1893, but I can't find anything for Jess or the twins.'

'You're calling her Jess as though you know that's the name she went by.'

'It's what's written on the back of the painting I took this photo of,' Nat said, pointing to the Polaroid. 'Along with the year 1891.'

Tayte picked up the photograph. It was attached to a copy of Jessie Bates's birth record. The image was small, but sharp, and the closer he brought it to his eyes to study it, the less sense it made. It was like no other portrait he had ever seen. It was a colourful abstract, made up of small blocks of various shapes, that when viewed up close resembled little more than the perhaps confused and chaotic mind of the artist. From a distance, however, everything fell into place, and he saw a young, fair-haired girl in a plain white gown, with what he thought was a somewhat lost expression on her face. He thought it certainly fitted Nat's notion that the girl had just vanished – from the records at least.

'Well,' Tayte began, having given the matter some thought. 'On one record here, the 1891 census, we have a family consisting of a husband and wife, and their five children. On the other record, dated just two years later, we see that two of the children are living in an orphanage. It seems that something must have happened to the family between those years – for two of the children to wind up in an orphanage, I mean.'

'That's exactly what I thought,' Nat said. 'Maybe whatever happened could explain what became of Jess.'

Tayte ran a hand back through his hair, still thinking. 'How about adoption?' he asked. 'The two babies – the twins – might have gone to another family after whatever happened to separate them. Perhaps the same was true for Jess.'

Nat was drawing air through her teeth long before Tayte finished speaking. 'I did look.'

'No good?'

Nat shook her head.

'I'm not surprised,' Tayte said. 'Adoptions can be tough to find – sometimes impossible. Especially when you're looking back past 1927, when the Adopted Children Register was created.' He paused and gave Nat a knowing smile. 'Thankfully, however, there are other ways.'

Nat returned his smile. 'I was so hoping you'd say that.'

'We can't rule out that something might have happened to Jess, though,' Tayte quickly added. 'And as a result she simply went missing. I wouldn't get your hopes up for her just yet. It wasn't entirely uncommon for children to vanish from the streets of Victorian London.'

'I understand,' Nat said. 'But however this turns out, I'd like to know.' She began to flick at her stud again. 'You will help me then?'

'That all depends.'

'On what?'

'On whether you're going to tell me what you're holding back.'

'How do you mean?'

Tayte had been duped into taking assignments before; some of them had turned into dangerous assignments that he might not have become involved in had he known all the facts up front.

'I mean, I'm sensing there's more to what you're telling me here,' he said. 'Most people interested in their family history want to trace their direct lineage first and foremost, and yet here you are, keen to find out more about the girl in your painting, who may or may not be one of your two-times-great-grandfather's sisters.' He picked up one of the records from the desk. 'I noticed this family tree you've started. It has a lot of holes in it.' He held it up. 'There's very little here on your maternal side, and yet you've gotten yourself hung up on a possible two-times-great-grandaunt. Before I decide whether or not to help you with your brick wall, I think it's fair that you tell me exactly why Jess is so important to you? If it's simply because you're intrigued by the painting you have and want to know more about the subject, I'll understand that. But if there's another reason, something more urgent perhaps, then I'd like to hear it.'

Nat began to blush. She let out a long, slow breath. 'I am intrigued about her because of the painting,' she said, 'but you're right. There's more to it – quite a lot more to it, actually. My mother left the painting to me. She died a few years ago while I was at uni. She had cancer.'

'I'm sorry to hear that.'

Nat gave a melancholy smile. 'It devastated me. My father left us when I was ten. My mother continued to bring me up by herself. Over the years that followed we became more like best friends. Then she got sick.'

Nat paused and looked away, again flicking nervously at her lip stud.

'You don't have to tell me all this,' Tayte offered, seeing how upset she was becoming.

Nat sniffed back her emotions. 'It's okay,' she said. 'You're right. It is fair that I tell you everything. That's how I came to own the painting, and our little terraced house in Spitalfields. I dropped out of uni to take care of my mum at home while I could. Then I suddenly found myself alone. I think that's why I became interested in my family history. Knowing who my ancestors were somehow made me feel less alone, if that makes sense.'

'Oh, it makes perfect sense,' Tayte said, wondering whether that was his reason, too. He'd never known either of his biological parents, having been abandoned as a baby.

'After my mum died, I found myself with plenty of time on my hands, too. I'd lost all interest in university, and I had to do something.' She laughed to herself. 'I was going to become an architect, now I'm a part-time Uber cab driver.'

'And already something of an amateur genealogist,' Tayte said. 'I take it the painting of Jess has been in your family a while?'

Nat nodded. 'Quite a while, yes,' she said. 'I never asked Mum how she came by it, but I've always thought of it as a family heirloom. She always kept it on the wall above the gas fire in the living room, where it was still hanging until recently.'

From Nat's darkening expression, Tayte knew it wasn't still hanging there now because she'd simply moved it.

'It was stolen,' Nat continued. 'And that's not all.'

Tayte's curiosity was piqued, along with his wariness. 'Go on.'

'My cousin's flat in Holborn was broken into the same week, just a few days earlier. It was during the day. Whoever broke in must have thought the occupants would be out at work, which they usually are, but my cousin, Trisha, wasn't feeling well and had called in sick. The police told me they thought she must have disturbed the burglar, and he most likely panicked and shoved her out of the way as he fled. Trisha fell and hit her head. The burglar probably didn't even know it at the time, but she wound up in hospital with a severe head injury. She died during the night.'

Tayte's heart sank. 'I'm so sorry,' he said. 'That's just terrible. And you say a few days after that your house was also broken into and the painting of Jess was stolen?'

'That's right. Whoever killed my cousin, intentionally or otherwise, must have gone there first looking for the painting, surely?'

It seemed highly likely to Tayte. The coincidence was certainly too big to ignore. 'Was anything stolen from your cousin's house?'

'Nothing.'

'And was anything else stolen from your house besides the painting?'

'No, just the painting,' Nat said. 'Whoever took it knew exactly what he was after.'

'So it seems,' Tayte said, wondering who might want such a thing and why. It was an abstract painting of a rather plain-looking young girl from the late Victorian era – a family heirloom, perhaps. 'Did the police tie the break-ins together?'

'Sort of,' Nat said. 'They told me they couldn't rule

out a connection, but when I last enquired they still had no leads.'

'I see,' Tayte said, reaching without awareness into his jacket pocket for a Hershey's Miniature to help him think, but all he found in there were empty wrappers. 'I understand now why you're so interested in the girl in that painting. Through learning more about Jess, you hope to find out who killed your cousin.' Having heard all that Nat had to say about the matter, he wanted to know more about Jess now, too.

And about the painting.

'That's about it,' Nat said. 'So, now I've told you everything, will you help?'

As dark as the matter was, Tayte had to smile to himself. This kind of assignment seemed to have a way of finding him, even now, it seemed. He'd given up working in the field for the regular, relatively uneventful hours that teaching offered, and yet here he was again, about to agree to help someone with their genealogical brick wall, knowing full well that someone had been murdered, in all likelihood in connection with it. Yes, he was going to help. If he were honest with himself, he'd missed the fieldwork far too much to say no, despite the possible dangers. He nodded, and Nat's face beamed.

'Great!' she said with a little jump. 'So, where do we go from here?'

'You go home, and so do I,' Tayte said, glancing up at the clock on the wall over the door. 'Do you mind if I hang on to your records for now? I'd like to go over them.'

'Keep them as long as you like.'

'Thanks,' Tayte said, gathering them up. 'Okay then,' he added a moment later. 'Can we meet back here at ten o'clock tomorrow morning? As it's Thursday tomorrow, we'll have the place to ourselves until after lunch.'

'Sure,' Nat said. 'I can't wait.'

As Tayte finished gathering Nat's records together, he studied the photograph of the painting again. It was the only real clue they had as to what was going on, although there was Jess herself, of course. As he began to slide Nat's records back into their folder, his mind started to drift as he wondered who Jess was, what she was like, and what had become of her. How had her portrait come to be painted, and by whom? And why had someone seemingly gone to great lengths to find it and steal it all these years later and, as it turned out, to kill for it?

CHAPTER TWO

North Kensington, London
1891

Jessie Bates lived in a narrow two-up, two-down terraced house on Pottery Lane. She shared a cramped room with her sister, Hannah, who was nine, her little brother, Charlie, who had just turned six, and the twins, who had been born in the bathtub eight months ago. Their mother, Gertrude, whose face was lined beyond her years, had very little time for any of them. She felt as though she had done her bit, carrying them each in her womb for nine months before pushing them out into the world.

'Don't expect me to wait on you as well!' she would often tell them, so, as the eldest, it fell to Jess to play mother to them all.

Their father, Harry, didn't have much to say about anything, which was a good thing because when he did speak it usually meant someone was in trouble. Jess did recall him once saying that they should all be grateful for their humble lodgings in the Potteries and Piggeries, as the district was called.

'We're lucky to have an entire house to ourselves at all,' he'd said one evening, drunk on gin, as he often was, although he'd been in one of his rare better moods. 'We're blessed indeed that we are not forced to sleep with our tired bodies slumped across rope beds in a doss house. In the second place, we're all the more fortunate to live at the Potteries end of the street. Why, the houses at the Piggeries end stink to high heaven!'

He'd laughed and laughed at that, his loose jowls quivering like jellies, but Jess hadn't believed him – not about the stink. She did feel fortunate to have a roof over her head, of course, and that she only had to share a room with her siblings, however many came and went, but as for the smell... She knew the Potteries and Piggeries district was all one and the same these days, and she couldn't imagine anywhere smelling worse than their house did, whichever end of the street it was on. The summer heat seemed to make everything smell ten times worse, too, although the winter brought with it other problems.

'If it wasn't for Mr Butterfill's good grace,' Harry had said, singling Jess out as he'd spoken, 'things might be very different indeed. We would all of us do well to keep that in mind, don't you agree, Jess?'

Jess was reflecting on that very conversation now, not least because Mr Butterfill's name had cropped up again. Harry had gathered everyone together for a chat, which he hardly ever did, so she knew it had to be important. She was sitting against the wall in the downstairs front room, beneath the open window for the breeze, wearing the only dress she had. Much like her skin, it was more brown than white with dirt, the formerly pretty lace trim long since tattered and torn. She'd tied up her hair with a piece of string she liked, which was the next best thing in lieu of a colourful ribbon, but she'd given the last length of ribbon she'd found to Hannah. None of the

Bates children were wearing shoes, which often resulted in splinters from the rough floorboards. There were only two chairs in the entire house, and they were strictly for the grown-ups. Her father was in an old, cracked leather wing chair, while her mother had pulled up beside him a fragile-looking Windsor chair. Hannah was to Jess's left, little Charlie to her right, and the twins were upstairs asleep in the back room. As usual, it wasn't their father doing the talking, but their mother.

'Mr Butterfill says he needs to put the rent up,' Gert said, pulling at her wiry red hair, which Jess had noticed her mother often did when she was in her father's close company. 'He says he can fit more families into a house like this by renting them a room apiece.'

Jess saw a snarl creep across her father's face at the thought. She also noticed that his dark eyes were, for reasons she did not yet know, fixed on her all the while her mother was speaking.

'I don't earn nearly enough at the match works to make up the difference he's asking for, let alone pay the rent we already owe him,' Gert continued, looking at Harry, 'and your poor dad's leg won't let him do much these days, but he has a plan, isn't that right, Harry love?'

Harry gave no more than a small nod in reply, seemingly distracted, his eyes further narrowing on Jess, as if waiting to see her reaction to what was coming. Was she to be sent out to work at the match works, too? If so, she would have welcomed it, were it not for the fact that there would be no one other than her father left at home to look after the twins, and that was unthinkable, so what could she do about Mr Butterfill's demands? The way her father was staring at her, however, told Jess that his plan did somehow concern her.

'Your dad and Mr Butterfill have talked the matter over,' Gert said, also now looking directly at Jess, her features bearing a rare look of sympathy, 'and they've reached an agreement.'

Jess found herself sitting up a little now, as she waited to hear what that agreement was. She would have spoken out, asked there and then, had she not known better. You did not speak at times like this unless you were invited to do so, which was hardly ever.

Gert cleared her throat. 'Mr Butterfill has shown himself to be a most reasonable man,' she said, pulling harder at her hair as she looked away from Jess, down at the dusty floorboards. 'He has, for some time now, taken a particular liking to our Jess and, in lieu of the extra rent money, and what we already owe him, has graciously agreed to marry her.'

Jess drew a sharp breath. Her mouth hung open, ready to speak out regardless, but her father's black look warned her not to.

'Furthermore,' Gert continued, her eyes now wandering around the room without settling on anything, first to the patch in the wall by the door where the plaster had long since fallen in, and then to the soot-blackened fireplace that was little more than a dark and cheerless hole. She cleared her throat again. 'Furthermore,' she repeated, forcing a more assertive tone, 'Mr Butterfill has agreed to pay your dad a handsome amount on top. There'll be enough to clear all his debts, and plenty besides. Enough to put food in my poor babies' mouths for some time to come.' She looked at Jess again now. 'You want that for them, dear, don't you?'

Jess did want that for them, but not like this. She was not yet ready to marry anyone, and certainly not Mr

Butterfill, who had to be at least forty years her senior.

'You're twelve now, Jess,' Gert continued. 'With our consent it's all legal and above board. Your dad is also of the opinion that it will safeguard our future here. After all, Mr Butterfill could hardly turn us out on the street if he was one of the family, now could he?'

Jess didn't particularly care what happened to her parents. She had no affection for her father, and very little for her mother, not least because so little was ever given. She despised her mother all the more now, though, for using Hannah, Charlie and the twins like this, knowing full well that she would do anything for them. She wanted to say that she thought her proposed marriage to Mr Butterfill was a hideously cruel idea. She wanted to ask them to find another way, but what good would it do? Her father had already agreed to sell her to Mr Butterfill – she could see it no other way – just as he had agreed to sell little Charlie to the sweep.

She looked at her father again, wondering whether this had been his plan for her for some time. He had lost his job as a night-man, emptying cesspits, months ago, which was why they had fallen behind with the rent. He had blamed some trouble with his leg as the reason, which was also apparently why he'd been unable to secure another job since, but Jess had never seen him try. And why should he, when he'd seen how Mr Butterfill had taken such a fancy to her? Why bother, when there was easier money to be made? The way she saw it, she was the only reason Mr Butterfill had not already turned them out on to the street. She was the only reason they were not already spending their nights hung over rope beds in the doss house.

Jess's hesitancy in replying to her mother's question

caused Harry to sit forward and scowl at her. She saw his hand move down to his side, and she knew what that meant. Harry's father had been a gamekeeper's assistant. When the quarry was brought down, it was his job to dispatch any wounded prey with what was known as a gamekeeper's priest – a short, hard cudgel, often made from antler or, in this case, of woven leather, eight inches long, with a wrist strap at one end and a bulbous lead weight at the other. Harry had told Jess once how his father used to beat him with it. Now he used it to beat them. At least, he used it on little Charlie most of the time, which made Jess wonder now whether he did so because he didn't want to spoil his girls – didn't want to damage the goods he intended to sell into marriage as soon as they were old enough.

'Girl!' Harry snarled, the only verbal warning she would get.

Jess nodded, and Harry settled back again.

Through blackened, broken teeth, Gert began to smile. 'That's my Jess,' she said. 'Always putting others first. Mr Butterfill will be delighted. He's agreed to take you in straight away, so your dad can pay off his debts all the sooner. No need to wait for the banns to be read. He'll be along tomorrow.'

CHAPTER THREE

Tomorrow...

Lying in bed with Hannah fast asleep beside her, Jess could not get that word out of her head. Tomorrow, tomorrow, tomorrow... Mr Butterfill was coming to take her away.

'So soon,' she said under her breath.

Her thoughts drifted as she imagined what her life might be like with the aging Mr Butterfill for a husband. The only solace she could find was that, as he was already in his fifties, he was perhaps not many more years for this world, so the days she would have to endure with him could be short-lived. But what of her siblings? She worried for them. Perhaps they would be better off without her there to look out for them. With more money available as a result, their lives would be all the better for it. But how would they cope? The twins were still very young, and she supposed Hannah would just have to step up, as she had had to. Hannah would soon be ten, after all.

Yes, with more money for better food and clothing, and coal for the fire in the winter, they would be all right. The picture seemed rosy enough to Jess. By marrying Mr Butterfill, she would be helping them immeasurably. Surely it was a small sacrifice to pay on her part? She pictured her father gambling it all away then, which was how he'd managed to land himself in so much debt in the first place, or drinking it away on gin and beer with her mother, and the rosy picture she had painted for her siblings began to sour.

She was unable to dwell further on the matter, however, because she was suddenly aware of faint voices in the chimney. She thought it was one of the neighbours at first, getting into a row, as they often did, or someone out in the street – a prostitute or a drunk, or perhaps some stranger to the area without the good sense to know that Notting Dale was not a safe place to be out wandering at night – but the voices sounded closer. They were familiar, too. She sat up and listened more closely. One of the voices belonged to her father, down in the front room. There was someone else there, too, but the voices were still too faint to make out what was being said. Had Mr Butterfill come already – come to steal her away with him in the dead of night? She had to find out, so she got up and crept to the top of the stairs, mindful to avoid the holes in the floor and the creakiest of the floorboards. At the top of the narrow staircase, she could hear the voices more clearly.

'A little more time, gentlemen,' she heard her father say. 'A few days at most. That's all I ask.'

'Why should we believe you this time?' someone else said, his tone guttural and flat.

'Yeah,' came another voice, deeper and more gravelly still. 'You've been stringing us along for weeks. Time's up, Harry.'

Jess was glad to know that her father wasn't talking to Mr Butterfill, but she was concerned nonetheless. The other voices belonged to the Fuller brothers, Frank, who had spoken first, and John. They were the only people

Jess knew of who seemed to put the fear of God into her father whenever they had reason to call. Everyone in Notting Dale, perhaps the whole of London, either knew them or knew of them, and woe betide anyone who borrowed from them and couldn't pay them back. There was no sanctuary to be found in the debtors' prison for those wretched souls. The only peace they would find was at the bottom of the Thames.

'And just how is it you expect to be in a position to pay us back in a few days?' Frank asked. 'If you ain't got no money now, how will you come by it?'

'Had a win on the gee-gees, have you?' John chipped in, laughing a little. 'Last we heard, you ain't got no more than two farthings to rub together.'

Frank laughed, too. 'Must have been some rotten old nag to get odds enough to pay us back, Harry.'

'It's not the horses, gents,' Harry said. 'It's my daughter, Jess. You remember her, don't you? My eldest? Proper treat on the eyes, she is.'

'What about her?' Frank said, and Jess found herself moving down the stairs a few steps.

'I have an arrangement with the landlord of this here building – Mr Butterfill,' Harry said. 'Perhaps you've heard of him.'

It went quiet for a few seconds, and Jess wondered why neither of the Fuller brothers answered her father. Surely they either knew him, or they did not?

'Go on,' Frank said, and there was something about the way he drew the words out that told Jess they had heard of him. She sensed it was not in a good way.

'Well,' Harry said. 'He's going to take Jess off our hands. Promised to marry her, too, he has. In return, he's agreed to keep the rent down, and pay me enough – more than enough, in fact – to settle my debts with you fine fellows.'

'Are you taking the piss?' John said, and Jess imagined his thick neck jutting forward as he pushed his face aggressively in front of her father's.

'H-however do you mean?' Harry said, stammering a little, which he never ordinarily did.

'I mean,' John said, 'that there ain't nothing fine about us, and you know it.'

'You misunderstand,' Harry said, laughing nervously. 'I simply meant to imply that it's a fine thing you're doing, giving me more time to pay what I owe you, that's all.'

'Who said you had more time?' Frank asked. 'Did you, John?'

'I did not, Frank,' John said.

'No, I didn't think so.'

'But surely,' Harry said, 'I've just told you, Mr Butterfill is going to pay me a handsome sum for Jess, any time now. What's a few more days, as long as you get your money? With interest, of course,' Harry quickly added.

'Oh, of course,' Frank said. 'What do you think, John? Shall we give Harry more time?'

'I don't know, Frank. I can't say I'm happy with where he's getting the money from.'

'No,' Frank said, 'me neither. The likes of Butterfill leave a particularly unpleasant taste in the mouths of more principled sorts such as ourselves.'

'Yeah, we got principles,' John said. 'Still, money is money, Frank.'

'Very true, John. Very true.'

'Mr Butterfill?' Harry said, sounding perplexed.

John scoffed. 'Don't pretend you don't know what he's

about. He's taken in girls like your Jess before, and you know it. I'll wager he told their fathers he was going to marry them, too, but he's never married a single one of them.'

'And where are they now, eh?' Frank said. 'I ask you that, Harry. Where are they now?'

Sitting halfway down the stairs by now, Jess could feel her heart pounding in her chest. What did he mean? What other girls? What had happened to them indeed? She wondered then what would happen to her if she went with Mr Butterfill, as her father had arranged. She could think of no good coming from it, and certainly not marriage, it seemed. Did her father really know all this, as the Fuller brothers were suggesting? She thought he did. A moment later, he confirmed it.

'Look,' Harry said. 'Whatever Mr Butterfill's faults, what's done is done. He's taken a liking to Jess and we've reached an agreement in the matter. I need the money, don't I? What was I to do?'

There was a long silence, during which Jess imagined the Fuller brothers studying her father, as if asking what kind of despicable creature would do such a thing. At least, that was the question on Jess's lips.

'Your own daughter,' Frank said. 'You don't deserve a family, Harry. You really don't.'

'We'll see you soon,' John said.

A moment later, Jess heard their heavy footsteps on the floorboards as they began to leave, and she crept quickly but quietly back up to her room. By the time she got back into bed beside Hannah, her imagination was already running wild with dark thoughts of the life that Mr Butterfill had in store for her.

Whatever was she to do?

CHAPTER FOUR

Tap! Tap! Tap!

'Oh my Lord, it's him! I know it's him!' Jess said, bouncing the twins faster in her arms, until first one, and then the other began to cry. 'I'm sorry, lambs,' she said. 'I can't help it, see. He's come for me and I don't want to go with him.'

She heard her father stomping down the stairs. It was early evening, not quite dark out, and he'd been taking a nap. Her mother was not yet home from the match works, and Hannah and Charlie had been sent outside while she stayed in to keep the twins quiet.

Tap! Tap! Tap!

'All right! All right! I'm coming!' Harry called down. 'Jess? Where the blazes are you? Didn't you hear the door?'

How could Jess not hear it? She had been listening intently for it ever since she heard the brass tip of Mr Butterfill's walking cane on the pavement outside, hoping he would pass by. The sound of it tapping on the door now instilled so much fear in her that she found herself shrinking back into the far corner of the room, forgetful of the damp that had rotted several of the floorboards there. The twins were still crying in her arms, but she was insensible to their din. All she could hear was the tap, tap, tapping, and the voices in her head telling her that all was not as it seemed with Mr Butterfill. She took another step back and one of the rotten floorboards threatened to give way beneath her, tipping her balance. It immediately brought her back to her senses.

'Shh…' she said to the twins, bouncing them again. 'There, there. It's all right. I'm just a bit nervous, that's all. I didn't expect Mr Butterfill to come so soon.'

Neither, it seemed, did Jess's father. She heard him lift the catch and open the door, and she imagined he was ready to give whoever was out there an earbashing for disturbing his sleep. That was until he saw who was there. Then he would step back and meekly bow his head, just as he always did when Mr Butterfill called.

'Why, Mr Butterfill,' Harry said. 'I didn't expect you for a couple more days yet. Come in, come in.'

Jess heard the front door close with a thud.

'Will you be taking Jess with you now, then?' she heard her father ask. 'Is that it?'

'I will not,' Butterfill said, his haughty tone setting the two men apart. 'Not today, that is. Today, I merely wish to see the girl.'

'Right you are, Mr Butterfill,' Harry said, 'and judging from all that blubbering coming from the front room, I'd say she was in there with the twins.' He laughed awkwardly. 'What babies have to cry about, I do not know,' he added. 'Follow me, won't you?'

The door Jess had been staring at for the past few minutes suddenly shot open and she drew a sharp breath, which she held on to as her father brought Mr Butterfill in. He was a tall, rangy man, who Jess had always thought looked as if he could afford to eat better than he did. A pair of round glasses were pinched to the bridge of his not inconsiderable nose, which Jess thought was well suited to looking down at the likes of them. He was stooping as he came into the room, on account of his top hat, which he removed, sniffing the air with a sour expression as he did so. It prompted him to take a handkerchief from his lapel pocket and wave it in front of his face without delay. The twins, who were by now growing heavy in Jess's arms, fell silent as soon as he entered.

'Here she is,' Harry said, extending an arm towards Jess. 'I'd have had her scrub up a bit if I'd known you was coming.'

Butterfill approached Jess, and his brisk movement set the candle flame dancing. He drew a long breath through his nose, tilting his head back slightly as his eyes took Jess in more fully. 'We'll soon get you cleaned up, my dear,' he said, speaking softly to her, the corners of his mouth lifting in just the hint of a smile.

Jess didn't say a word. She knew it wasn't her place to, but more than that, she didn't want to, not out loud. Inside her head, however, she was saying plenty.

Where are you going to take me? What are you going to do with me? Will anyone ever see me again?

'But where are my manners?' Harry said. 'Can I get our Jess here to fetch you something to drink? There's beer, gin, or maybe this calls for a drop of the good stuff, eh?'

'No,' Butterfill said. 'That won't be necessary.'

Harry gave a low harrumph. 'Well, if you're sure. I don't offer the good stuff to just anyone. Got a fine bottle of—'

Butterfill put his hand up to stop Harry talking. 'I did not call to socialise with you, Mr Bates,' he said. A moment later he made Jess jump as he reached out and held her by the chin. He began to turn her face to the left and to the right, as if she were nothing more than a piece of fruit at a market stall. 'Now, are you absolutely certain the girl is...' He trailed off as if fishing for the right word. 'Unspoiled?' he added, talking to Harry, yet not taking his eyes off Jess for a moment.

'Quite certain, yes,' Harry said.

'Only quite certain?' Butterfill snapped, his nose creasing with annoyance at the notion that Jess was anything but unspoiled.

Harry laughed nervously to himself again. 'That is to say, I am most positively certain.'

'And how is that?' Butterfill asked.

'Well, I,' Harry began, but he stopped, seemingly flummoxed as to how he could honestly answer such a question.

'You cannot be sure, can you, Mr Bates?'

Harry's face began to redden. 'Why, I give you my word, Mr Butterfill. My Jess is the purest girl in Notting Dale.'

Butterfill snorted. 'That, sir, is saying very little.' He leaned in closer to Jess. 'Tell me, my dear, are you as pure as your father would have me believe?'

Jess wondered whether an easy way out of this would be to lie and say she wasn't, but she did not think there would be anything easy about what would follow from her father as soon as Mr Butterfill left. She thought her father would likely beat her senseless with that gamekeeper's priest of his. She wasn't comfortable with lying anyway. Lies usually only led to more trouble than they were worth.

'Begging your pardon Mr Butterfill, sir,' she said, 'but yes, sir, I am. Pure as these little lambs here in my arms.'

The corners of Butterfill's mouth lifted higher as Jess

spoke. 'I'm delighted to hear it,' he said. Then whispering to her, he added, 'Besides, I shall find out for myself soon enough, shan't I?'

His words sent a chill through Jess. She felt herself beginning to shake as fear rose inside her. Then Butterfill turned his back to her, and she was glad to see it.

'If the pair of you are lying to me,' Butterfill told Harry as he went back to the door, 'it will be the worse for you and your family. Do you understand?'

'Of course, Mr Butterfill,' Harry said, 'but there's no need for any concern in the matter, I assure you.'

'Good,' Butterfill said, stooping again as he donned his top hat to leave. 'That's very good indeed. Have her ready in two days. She must bring nothing with her.'

CHAPTER FIVE

Present day

The morning after Tayte met Nat Cooper, he was on his foldaway bicycle again, heading back through the busy streets of London to the Marcus Brown School of Family History. He'd agreed to meet her there at ten o'clock, but he was running late, and for good reason, to his mind. After spending much of what remained of the previous evening fruitlessly poring over Nat's records, looking for a way to discover more about the girl in the painting, he'd awoken that morning with an idea he'd felt compelled to pursue, and he was keen to share the results with her.

He stuck out his arm and hurriedly turned a corner, his wheels wobbling beneath him as he did so, his briefcase bouncing on the bungee cord that was slung over his shoulder. He steadied the bicycle and checked his watch. It was an Apple smartwatch that, like the bicycle, had also been given to him with fitness in mind, but he only really used it to tell the time. The retro red LED digits on the watch face, which he'd chosen because the style reminded him of the 1980s digital watch he once owned and had been so fond of, told him he was a full twenty minutes late.

'I hope you waited,' he said under his breath as the building that housed the school came into view.

He brought his bicycle to a hard stop outside, and the brakes emitted their signature rubbery squeal as he juddered to a halt. Between two parked cars he dismounted, panting as usual. As he began to fold the bicycle away, he saw Nat sitting on the step, her attire as colourful as before. It instantly put a smile on his face. For a moment he found himself wondering whether a little colour to contrast with his perennially tan linen suits and white shirts wouldn't go amiss – some colourful socks, perhaps – but the moment soon passed.

'Good morning!' he called to her. 'I'm sorry I'm late, but I think you'll soon agree the wait was worth it.'

'Good morning, Mr Tayte,' Nat said, getting to her feet as Tayte approached her. 'Have you found something?'

Tayte thought the cheery, sing-song manner of her greeting made him sound every bit the schoolteacher. 'JT,' he said with a smile. 'Please call me JT. And yes, maybe I have found something. That is, I've had an idea that could turn into something. Let's go up and I'll tell you all about it,' he added, unlocking the door.

Nat swung her red shoulder bag around and stooped to pick something up. 'Here, I bought you a coffee,' she said, holding up two paper cups bearing the Starbucks logo. 'I don't know how you take it, so I got black to be on the safe side. I hope it's still warm.'

'You're an angel,' Tayte said, smiling as they went inside. 'Black is just perfect. Did you pick up any sugar?'

'No, sorry. I'll remember next time.'

'That's okay,' Tayte said. 'There's a secret stash I share with the art master up in the desk drawer.'

Inside the room, Tayte set his briefcase and his coffee

down on the desk, and then he unfolded two of the chairs for them to sit on. He wasn't teaching today, so he didn't want to assume the role of teacher by sitting on the comfier chair at his desk opposite Nat. She wasn't there as a student today, either. They were partners, working on an assignment together – Nat's assignment about the life of a girl called Jessie Bates, and an abstract portrait someone had painted of her. The burning question on Tayte's mind that morning was no longer so much about the subject of the portrait, however, but who the artist was.

Tayte took out Nat's photograph of the painting from his briefcase, knocked back half his coffee, which was by now barely lukewarm, and set the cup down again. They sat down. Attached to the photograph this time was not a copy of Jessie Bates's birth certificate, but three other images. Tayte first handed the photograph of the painting to Nat, keeping hold of the other images for now.

'I found your research to be very thorough,' he said, 'but, as you discovered, there's nothing in there to offer any new direction when it comes to finding out what happened to Jess. By the time I'd gone over everything, I knew we had to find another way, which, of course, is the very nature of genealogical brick walls. Sometimes you have to find a way around them. In this case, I think the painting itself is our best way forward. Your photograph of the painting, that is.'

Nat was studying it. 'How can this help us? I must have looked at it a thousand times.'

'The artist,' Tayte said. 'It stands to reason that whoever painted this portrait of Jess had to know her on some level. Due to the abstract nature of the image, it's hard to make out too much of the subject detail, but this plainly dressed young girl hardly seems the model type. I don't think the artist found her at any kind of agency.'

'No,' Nat agreed, shaking her head as she continued to take the photograph in. 'You think he knew her then?'

'I think he must have. Maybe a little. Maybe a lot. It might not come to much, but it's something I'd like to explore.'

'The artist,' Nat mused. She looked up from the photograph. 'I have no idea who that was.'

'I didn't think so,' Tayte said. 'I'll bet you never saw a name on the canvas, did you?'

Nat shook her head.

'That's because it's lost in the abstract,' Tayte offered. 'It's hard to see in the photograph, and on the original painting, I suspect, but there's a letter in every corner apart from the bottom left. Reading them from the upper left corner to the right then down, they spell out the name, or the initials, SEB.'

Nat began to squint as she looked for them. 'I can't see anything.'

Tayte laughed. 'I'm not surprised. They're too small, and you're too close. Here.' He handed Nat one of the other images. 'Whenever I can't make out the words and dates on a headstone, I take a digital photo of it. I can then enlarge and enhance it on my laptop, and suddenly everything becomes much clearer. I took a digital photo of your photo, and then I blew it up and enhanced it. I still couldn't see anything. In fact, it just made the whole thing more abstract. It wasn't until I was walking back to my laptop from a good distance that one of the letters jumped out at me. Even with the original, I suspect you'd have to know what you were looking for to see them.'

Nat's face suddenly appeared enlightened. A smile drifted across her dark cherry lips as she took in the first image and saw what Tayte had seen. 'There it is,' she said. 'The letter S.'

Tayte handed the other images to her. 'And here are the letters E and B.'

'SEB,' Nat said. 'Sebastian?'

'Could be,' Tayte offered. 'Or the artist's initials.'

'True,' Nat said with a nod. 'So, either way, who was SEB?'

'That, Nat, is the million-dollar question. To answer it, I think we may need greater knowledge of the art world than either of us possesses.'

Nat pulled her shoulder bag up on to her lap and took out a small laptop. 'There must be hundreds of art experts here in London,' she said. 'Someone must know who SEB was.'

'Perhaps,' Tayte said. 'If his work amounted to anything. But your portrait of Jess could have been painted by an unknown, or by an artist who fell into obscurity a long time ago.'

Nat started typing. 'It's worth a look,' she said, 'and I can't think of anywhere better to start than the group of galleries that share your name, albeit with a different spelling.'

'The Tate galleries,' Tayte said.

He pulled his chair around beside Nat so he could better see her screen. She was typing a query into a contact page, giving details of the painting and the name or initials Tayte had found. The website stated that specialist queries such as theirs would be forwarded to a relevant expert, who would usually respond directly. As Nat finished typing and sent the query, Tayte thought it sounded promising. There was no bigger art gallery network in England, although he was impatient to get things moving and he'd also noted that it could take up to five days to receive a reply.

Nat closed her laptop. 'Now I suppose we just have to wait for an answer.'

'And keep our fingers crossed,' Tayte said, wondering how he could speed up the process. A moment later, he went to the desk, opened his briefcase and took out his laptop. He sat down again. 'I didn't have time to check the Internet before I came here.' He pulled up a Google browser and typed 'SEB abstract artist' into the search field. The first few links were for sales advertisements, so he scrolled down. Then he saw a link to someone called Stephen Ebenezer Black. 'This looks promising,' he said as he clicked it.

'It says he's an artist,' Nat said, a hint of excitement rising in her tone. 'It could be him.'

'Yes, it could,' Tayte said. 'There's not much information here, though – no examples of his work to compare with, although he did paint abstracts.'

'He died relatively young, didn't he?' Nat said, reading the page alongside him.

Tayte nodded. 'Forty-nine years old,' he said. 'Born 1875, died 1924.'

There was nothing more to glean from the web page, so Tayte returned to his Google search and continued to scroll through several more pages of search results, yielding nothing of promise. He tried the artist's full name next, and then he saw something that looked very promising indeed. It was an image of an abstract painting that looked nothing like the portrait of Jess. It was a London cityscape – a skyline painting that, while still abstract, exhibited great detail. He might have ruled out that it was by the same artist were it not for the fact that the detail only really stood out because the image was small, as if he were viewing it from afar. That much it did have in common with Nat's painting of Jess. He clicked on the image and was taken to the website of the Tate Britain art museum.

'Well, what do you know?' Tayte said. 'We've come full circle. If this is the same artist who painted your portrait of Jess, there's another of his works right here in London.' He turned to Nat. 'It's a fine morning out there. How about a stroll to Millbank? Maybe we can take a closer look at it.'

'Perhaps it has the initials SEB in the corners,' Nat offered, raising her eyebrows.

'My thoughts exactly,' Tayte said. 'And if it does, maybe we can talk to someone about it, and more importantly, about Stephen Ebenezer Black.'

Nat snapped her laptop shut and shot to her feet. 'Let's go,' she said, packing it away in her bag before Tayte had taken another breath.

Tayte laughed to himself. 'That art museum isn't going anywhere,' he said, 'but I love your enthusiasm.' He stood up, a little less energetically. 'I'll get us some fresh, hot coffee along the way.'

CHAPTER SIX

Tate Britain's impressive neoclassical facade was in full sunlight when Tayte and Nat arrived at the wide stone steps that ran up to the main visitors' entrance. London's historic buildings never ceased to amaze Tayte, and he liked to appreciate them whenever he could. There were few cities in the world that could boast such architectural diversity, dating from the early 1600s right up to the modern buildings that always seemed to be in construction. He stopped momentarily to take in the gallery, gazing up at the high portico towards the pediment, which was topped with a proud statue of Britannia in the centre, a lion to her left, and a unicorn to her right. He thought about the Great Fire of 1666, how it had destroyed so much of the city, and yet out of the ashes it had paved the way for so much more. He was about to head up the steps when he felt a tug at his jacket. It was Nat.

'I've had a reply,' she said, holding up her phone.

'Already?' Tayte said. 'Whoever it's from must be as keen as we are. What does it say?'

Nat read the email. 'It's from someone called Barrett Huckabee. He says he thinks he can help us. There's a number to call.'

'Great. Do you want to call him or shall I?'

Nat tapped the number on her screen and handed her

phone to Tayte. 'You're probably better at this sort of thing than I am.'

Tayte pressed the phone to his ear and waited. A few seconds later, Huckabee picked up the call.

'Barrett Huckabee,' he said, and Tayte thought he sounded a little out of breath.

'Mr Huckabee,' Tayte said. 'Hi, my name's Jefferson Tayte. I'm calling about the Stephen Black painting. We just got your message to call you.'

'Mr Tayte!' Huckabee said, his tone suddenly bright and enthusiastic. 'Yes, as I said in my email, I believe I may be able to help you. Are you far from Millbank? I'll be at the gallery until around three this afternoon. I'm helping to set up a Turner exhibition.'

'You're at the Tate Britain gallery?' Tayte asked, looking up at the banners hanging between the pillars beneath the pediment. 'We're right outside. I saw they had one of Black's works here, so I thought we'd come over and ask someone about it.'

'Perfect!' Huckabee said. He laughed. 'You can ask me. Give me ten minutes and I'll come and find you. Perhaps you could wait for me in the main foyer?'

'We'll do that,' Tayte said. 'Thank you.'

He ended the call and handed Nat's phone back to her. 'Main lobby – ten minutes,' he said. 'He really is keen,' he added as they began to climb the steps. 'I can't wait to find out why.'

Inside the foyer they waited to one side of the main doors, where they could easily be seen yet were out of the way of the gallery visitors that came and went. It was a large, cool space, with a black-and-white mosaic floor, stone walls and pillars that supported the arched ceiling vaults. At the apex of each ceiling dome hung a series of matching globe chandeliers. There was nothing much at all by way of artwork or other ornamentation.

'Do you like art?' Nat asked Tayte as they waited.

Tayte had only ever owned one piece of genuine, original art, which, thanks to an old adversary, he no longer had. 'Sure,' he said. 'What's not to like? You?'

'I suppose so,' Nat said. 'I can't say I've really thought much about it before. That painting of Jess was just a part of the decor as I was growing up, until it was stolen. I've become a lot more interested in art since then.'

'Isn't that so often the way?' Tayte said. 'We don't always appreciate what we have until it's gone. I think that's one of those lessons we largely learn through experience.'

Nat gave a sombre nod. 'Well, I've certainly learned mine,' she said. She smiled. 'For now, at least.' A moment later, she asked, 'Have you been in London long?'

'Not too long,' Tayte said, wondering where the time had gone since he'd set up home in England. 'Almost two years now.'

'Did you meet someone? Is that what brought you here?'

Tayte didn't much care to talk about his private life, but neither did he wish to appear rude. 'My assignments brought me here,' he said, answering honestly, yet guardedly.

'Don't you miss your home country – your friends and family? I'm sure I would.'

'I miss going to a Redskins game every so often,' Tayte said. 'As for friends and family…' He trailed off. 'Let's just say that there's no one back home in America for me to miss.'

'So who's Marcus Brown?' Nat asked. 'I've been wondering since I came to see you yesterday and saw his name on the sign outside the school.'

Tayte didn't want to talk about Marcus Brown either, so he kept his answer brief. 'He was my friend,' he said. 'But he's gone now. He was a great genealogist – one of the best. There's not a day goes by that I don't miss him. I'm sure I could have appreciated him more than I did while he was alive.' He paused and gazed up at the lights. 'Like I said, some lessons we only seem to learn through experience, often when it's too late.'

'Mr Tayte!'

Tayte's thoughts snapped back to the present and he welcomed the interruption. He didn't want to get all melancholy about the past just now. He looked across the foyer and saw a young man with tidy brown hair, dressed in pale grey jeans and a black Metallica T-shirt, striding towards them. At first Tayte looked past him, expecting to see someone else – someone who more closely fitted the image he had in his mind of an art expert called Barrett Huckabee – but the only other people he could see had their backs to him, heading into the gallery. A moment later, Mr Metallica put his hand up, presumably having noticed that Tayte seemed to be looking for someone else.

'Are you Mr Tayte?' the man said as he approached, a broad smile on his youthful face.

Tayte put him somewhere in his mid-to-late twenties. The only thing about him that fitted the stereotypical image Tayte had formed in his mind ahead of meeting him was his Oxbridge elocution, and perhaps the glossy black shoes he was wearing, which would have looked very much at home beneath the hem of a fine pair of Savile Row suit trousers.

Tayte returned his smile. 'Jefferson Tayte,' he said, offering out his hand. He passed him a business card. 'This is Nat Cooper. It's her painting we've come to see you about.'

'Delighted to meet you both,' Huckabee said. 'Do excuse my attire,' he added. 'As I said, I've come in to help set up an exhibition we're hosting next week. Did you know that Tate Britain houses the largest Turner collection in the world?'

'I did not,' Tayte said.

Huckabee nodded. 'At his death, JMW Turner's bequest was to leave close to three hundred paintings and a great many sketches to the nation. There's a permanent rotating display of his work in the Clore Gallery, but every now and then Tate Britain holds a Turner exhibition to showcase more of his pieces together.' He paused, still smiling. 'But that's not why you're here, of course. Do you have the painting you mentioned in your message?' He looked them both up and down as he spoke, as if wondering whether it was concealed inside Nat's shoulder bag or Tayte's briefcase.

Nat spoke then. 'It was recently stolen from my house,' she said. 'I have a photograph, though. We'd like to learn more about the artist, if that's possible.'

'Oh dear,' Huckabee said. 'I'm sorry to hear that.'

Tayte took the photograph out from his briefcase and handed it to Huckabee.

'Unusual subject matter for S E Black,' he said, scrutinising the image. 'I've never seen anything like it from this particular artist, but the style is unmistakable. Very clever use of the abstract,' he added. 'How anyone can paint such detail at arm's length, which only comes together from a far greater distance, is beyond me. He's said to have been autistic – a savant. He was the only child of Ephraim and Eudora Black.' He handed the photograph back to Tayte. 'If you'd care to follow me, I'll show you one of his more celebrated paintings. It really is quite something.'

'Please lead on,' Tayte said, keen to see it.

Huckabee led them further into the art museum, through a pillared opening that led to a bright, wide flight of buff-tiled stairs. As they climbed, Tayte took in the large blocks of colour that had been painted on the walls around them, like an enormous Mondrian painting. At the top, through an open set of double doors, they entered one of the galleries. At once, Tayte saw the painting they had come to see. It was at the far end of the room. Having studied Nat's photo of Jess so much, and having seen a far smaller image of this particular skyline painting online earlier, he was in no doubt.

'I see you have a keen eye, Mr Tayte,' Huckabee said, clearly having noticed that Tayte had spotted it. 'S E Black painted this piece in 1902. The detail is incredible, wouldn't you say?'

'Even from this distance,' Nat said.

'Only from this distance,' Huckabee said. 'As we move closer, you'll see that the detail begins to break down until it falls into abstract. By the time we're standing in front of it, you'll struggle to find any kind of recognisable form.'

'The artist must have had a third eye,' Tayte said, still taking it in.

It was a large painting in a gilt frame, as was much of the artwork around him. This piece depicted a view from London's Southbank, looking across the Thames towards St Paul's Cathedral. The river and the bridges were bristling with detail, and the skyline itself, as it would have been around the turn of the twentieth century, appeared uncannily photographic.

Huckabee moved closer, and Tayte and Nat followed after him, their eyes locked on the painting, which lost its fine detail almost at once, just as Huckabee had said it would. By the time they were standing in front of it, the image made no sense at all, and the more Tayte stared at it, trying to find some semblance of familiarity, the more his eyes began to ache.

'If you look very closely in the bottom right-hand corner,' Huckabee said, 'you should be able to make out the letter B for Black, just as it appears on your painting.'

Tayte and Nat both looked together. As the painting was so large they had no trouble picking it out now they knew what to look for.

'The S and the E are in the upper corners, but you'll struggle to see them unless you climb a ladder or I take the painting down, which I can't do, of course.'

'We'll take your word for it,' Tayte said, fully satisfied that Nat's painting was created by the same artist.

'This painting,' Huckabee said, 'was bequeathed to the gallery by one of S E Black's descendants. It was the only S E Black painting still in the family at the time, and it caused quite a stir. He had four children, you see, and they were all rather put out by their father's gesture. They even tried to have his will overturned, but their appeal was without success. Who knows where the piece would be now if they had succeeded? Sold off into a private collection to split the proceeds of the sale, I imagine.'

'Perhaps that's why their father left it to the museum,' Tayte offered. 'He didn't want his kids fighting over it.'

'Quite,' Huckabee said. 'The eldest, Brendan Black, was strongly of the opinion that it should have been left to him, but all he received, along with his siblings, was a quarter share of their father's home and his fine art prints business. Black's Fine Art Prints, I seem to remember it being called. Not a particularly imaginative name.'

'Were there no other paintings in the family?' Nat asked.

Huckabee shook his head. 'S E Black was not particularly well known during his relatively short lifetime. Everything apart from this piece was sold off at one time or another. The exciting news is that his work became quite rare and valuable during the latter half of the last century.' He looked at Nat. 'I expect that would have been exciting news for you, had your S E Black painting not been stolen. A portrait by this artist is very unusual. I'm sure it would have fetched a small fortune at auction. The last sale I know of was in the 1980s, and that piece went for close to a million. Today, who knows?'

'No wonder someone wanted to steal it,' Tayte said.

'Someone who clearly knew its worth,' Huckabee added.

Tayte nodded, wondering who could have known not only what the painting was worth, but where it was, or at least, whose family it was in. From his albeit brief online search that morning, few results had been returned. This was not a well-known artist, and yet his work had garnered a wealthy following over the years since his death. All Tayte could determine for now was that certain art collectors would know its worth, if not its whereabouts, and in all probability, so would the artist's family.

'I don't suppose you know where any of Stephen Black's family live, do you?' Tayte asked. He thought it was time for him to follow his first rule of genealogy and go and talk to them if he could. He knew there were ways to at least identify them, through long hours of genealogical research, but he was hoping for a shortcut.

'I'm afraid not,' Huckabee said. 'Nor would I really be free to tell you if I did.'

'No, of course not,' Tayte said. 'I'm sorry I asked.'

'Not at all,' Huckabee said. 'It's always worth asking, isn't it?' He looked up at the painting again, and then at Tayte and Nat. 'It's such a shame your painting was stolen,' he said. 'I was very much looking forward to seeing it. Still, perhaps it'll turn up, eh?'

'I hope so,' Nat said.

Huckabee smiled at her. 'If it does, would you call me again?'

'I will,' Nat said.

'Good. In the meantime, if there's anything else I can help you with, please don't hesitate.'

'Thank you, Mr Huckabee,' Tayte said. 'You've been very helpful.'

As they left, Tayte took one last look back at the painting, in awe of the mind that had produced it, then as they took the stairs down again, he turned to Nat and said, 'I don't exactly know how just yet, but we need to find out where Stephen Black's descendants live and go pay them a visit.'

Nat winked at him. 'Don't worry,' she said. 'I'm already on it, and I have a plan.'

'You do? What is it?'

'Let's get back to the school and I'll show you.'

CHAPTER SEVEN

By the time Tayte and Nat arrived back at the Marcus Brown School of Family History, the seeds of several ideas had begun to germinate in Tayte's mind. Not least among them was the notion that one of S E Black's descendants had stolen Nat's painting and, in the process of finding it, had killed her cousin. He had wondered earlier who would know the value of such a painting, and its whereabouts. Now he began to wonder who even knew of its existence. Barrett Huckabee had told them that portraits were an unusual subject matter for S E Black, and that he'd never seen anything like it. Huckabee clearly had no knowledge of it until now, and neither, Tayte suspected, did the art world in general. 'Jess' was a hitherto unknown or lost piece.

This told Tayte that whoever stole the painting not only knew of its existence, but that the thief was probably close to the artist – close enough to know about 'Jess'. That person also knew in whose family he was likely to find the painting today, having systematically set about breaking into the homes of those family members while looking for it. This brought Tayte back to the idea that the artist knew his subject, perhaps well enough to give Jess the portrait he'd painted of her. Of course, it could have changed hands many times over the past century, but Nat had told him it had been in her family for some time. Were the two families connected in some way? Tayte was beginning to think they were. Whoever was behind this might have known that, or come to learn of the connection, perhaps through some genealogical research of their own.

Having heard what Barrett Huckabee had to say about the current Black family, the eldest son, Brendan Black, was right at the top of Tayte's list as far as motive was concerned. He'd clearly felt cheated out of his inheritance. He'd felt that the painting his father had bequeathed to the nation should have gone to him. Maybe he'd found another way to get his hands on one of his ancestor's paintings instead. Whatever was going on here, Tayte felt it all the more imperative that he and Nat should go and talk to the Black family if they could. As they set up at the main desk as before, he was keen to hear Nat's plan.

She took out her laptop as soon as they sat down. 'Companies House,' she said as the machine fired into life.

'Go on,' Tayte said, intrigued.

'Well, Barrett said—'

'Barrett? You're on first name terms already, are you?'

Nat blushed and Tayte laughed. 'I'm just teasing,' he said. 'Please continue. If you're going where I think you're going with this, you may be on to something.'

'The art expert,' Nat said, punctuating the words, a coy smile on her face, 'said that the Black family had a fine art prints business. If that's the case, it stands to reason that the business might be listed at Companies House.'

'Of course,' Tayte said. 'Good thinking.'

Nat brought up the government-run website. 'Find

company information,' she said as she clicked the link.

Tayte leaned in, reading down the list of information you could access for free. 'Registered address,' he said. 'It's at the top of the list.'

Nat nodded. 'Current and resigned officers could be useful, too. Huckabee said it was a family business.'

She clicked the 'Start now' button and was invited to search the register. Into the search field she typed the company name they were interested in, Black's Fine Art Prints. An exact match was shown at the top of the list, with an address not far away, in Lambeth. Nat clicked the link, and from the overview tab presented to them they learned that the private limited company was still active.

Tayte pointed to the third tab along. 'That looks promising.'

Nat clicked the 'People' tab, and there in front of them were four names: Brendan Black, whom they already knew about, a woman called Felicity Greenwood, Lawrence Black and Geoffrey Black. Beneath each name was listed a correspondence address, all of which were in London.

'Touchdown!' Tayte said, drawing the word out like an American football commentator.

'Their company roles are shown, too,' Nat said, indicating them on the screen. 'Brendan and Felicity are listed as directors, Lawrence and Geoffrey as secretaries.'

'Let's take a look at their filing history,' Tayte said, indicating another of the tabs. 'Maybe it'll tell us how well the business is doing.' By which he meant that it would perhaps give them a better picture of whether or not the family needed money.

Nat clicked the tab and they were presented with a

list of confirmation statements, unaudited abridged accounts, and other information. She clicked on the most recent accounts file and a PDF was displayed. She scrolled down and quickly came to the balance sheet. Tayte didn't need an accountant to tell him that Black's Fine Art Prints was in very bad shape.

'Ouch!' he said. 'That's not good at all. I'm surprised the company's still active.'

'There's certainly nothing here to suggest that anyone from this family doesn't need the money, is there?' Nat said. She went back to the names and addresses and started taking screenshots. 'Let's go and see them, shall we? Or at least try to.'

'It's the next logical step,' Tayte said, 'but I'm going to have to call it a day for now. I have my Friday and Saturday classes to prepare for.'

'Of course you do,' Nat said. She closed her laptop. 'How silly of me.'

'Not at all,' Tayte said. 'I love your enthusiasm. I'll be all prepped and ready by tomorrow afternoon. Let's meet back here then. Say three o'clock? There's no art class on Friday afternoons.'

'Great!' Nat said, getting to her feet. 'Who shall we try to see first?'

'How about the eldest, Brendan? I noticed his address also bore the company name. I suspect it's the store. Maybe he lives above it. That could be to our advantage on a Friday. We might stand a better chance of seeing the rest of the family over the weekend.'

Nat was nodding before Tayte had finished speaking. 'Tomorrow at three then,' she said, packing her laptop away. 'This is so exciting,' she added. 'I don't know how I'm going to sleep tonight.'

Tayte smiled back at her. If only she knew just how exciting some of his assignments had been during his last few years as a professional genealogist. 'You have a safe trip home,' was all he said in reply as he walked her to the door.

Alone with his thoughts, Tayte sat down at the desk, on the teacher side this time. He set up his laptop and took out the material he was working on for his Friday evening class, which he was currently running as a beginner class – a kind of genealogy 101 that covered all the basic concepts of discovering your family history. Saturday morning's class, on immigration, he could finish up in the morning. As he began, however, he found himself distracted by his earlier notion that whoever had stolen Nat's painting was somehow connected, not only with the artist, but also somehow with the subject.

He sat back in his chair and stared at the ceiling, for now unable to concentrate on his work. Like Nat, he had to concede that the life of the girl in the painting was beginning to take hold of him, just as the lives of the people in his assignments often did. To see the bigger picture, he knew he had to know more about her, and discover in what capacity she knew the artist, Stephen Ebenezer Black. He felt that was a key question, and he knew the answer had to be out there in the records somewhere. But where? How had their paths crossed all those years ago?

CHAPTER EIGHT

North Kensington, London
1891

Two days...

Jess didn't think Mr Butterfill had given her much time to say goodbye to her old life before he whisked her away to goodness knows what awaited her. She suspected, however, that her father had known this was coming for weeks, possibly months. She knew why he hadn't said anything until recently, too. He would have thought that if he'd told her sooner she would have tried to run away. Well, he was right there, Jess thought as she finished peeling another potato. She glanced back over her shoulder at the scullery door, to see if her father was still there. He'd put a padlock on the back door bolt soon after Mr Butterfill had left, which he never ordinarily did, and he'd been watching her like a hawk all day, presumably because there was no bolt on the front door. Her father wasn't there now, no doubt having become bored of watching her peel potatoes, or because his legs had grown tired, so she dropped the extra thick pieces of potato peel into her apron pocket for later.

Jess did not yet know how she would leave, being watched as closely as she was, but she knew she must.

She had hardly slept the night before, after Mr Butterfill had called in to see her, and she had thought about little else all night. How could she not at least try to run away? She had attempted to talk herself out of it several times, for little Charlie's sake, and for Hannah's and the twins', as she lay in the darkness, quietly crying to herself with frustration. No option she could come up with was entirely agreeable to her.

If she did run away, there would be no money, and Mr Butterfill would turn everyone out onto the street. What would become of her brother and her sisters then? If, on the other hand, she went with Mr Butterfill, what would become of her? She had already decided that it would end badly for her in some unthinkable way, as it seemingly had, according to the Fuller brothers, for countless other girls of Mr Butterfill's acquaintance. Now, too, she had seen for herself a glimpse of Mr Butterfill's lascivious intentions towards her. No, she could not be there when he came to collect her. As selfish as she felt about the matter, her brother and her sisters would simply have to make the best of it, as would she.

It was already afternoon now. Time was running out. She took off her apron and rolled it up. Then she opened one of the cupboards and tucked it out of the way behind the skillets for when her opportunity to leave arrived. She thought she could use it to carry a few provisions to go with her potato peelings: a small heel of bread perhaps, and a scrape of meat dripping from the dish one of the neighbours had been kind enough to give them. She went into the front room, where she found her father staring absently at the window, rapping his fingers on the arms of his chair, over and over again. It took him a moment to notice she had entered the room.

'Finished them spuds, have you?' he said, his eyes still fixed on the window, as if mesmerised by the dull glow from the daylight outside.

'Yes, Dad,' Jess said. 'We'll need more water to boil them. I'll go and fetch some in a minute, shall I?' It was a possible opportunity to escape. It meant she would have to go outside. If he agreed, she would simply keep going, past the water station, and never come back.

Harry, who hadn't once looked at Jess since she came into the room, looked at her now. He snapped his head around so sharply that he startled her. 'What, and leave the twins upstairs all by themselves? Why, your mother would never forgive me.'

Jess screwed her face up. 'I've left them here to fetch water hundreds of times.'

'Are you lipping me, girl?' Harry said, reaching a hand down beside him.

Jess knew he wouldn't dare beat her with that awful gamekeeper's priest of his the day before she was to go to Mr Butterfill, but she did not wish to test him. What good would it do, anyway? He was keeping her in, just as she suspected. She shook her head.

'Good!' Harry snapped. Then he relaxed again. 'Hannah and Charlie can go for it when they get home. I've sent them out with the broom – thought it was high time they made themselves useful.'

Jess had been sent out with the broom many times before, sweeping the crossings of filth for the ladies in the more well-to-do areas. On a good day, she had never brought more than a few pennies home. Most days she came home with nothing. She doubted Hannah and Charlie would fare any better. They were too young to compete in a trade that was dominated by rough boys at least twice their age. They would be bullied and moved on, as she often was.

'Talking of the twins,' Harry said, 'they've been quiet too long, don't you think? Perhaps you'd better go up and check on them.'

Jess sighed to herself as she turned and left. She began to close the front-room door on her way out, but her father stopped her.

'Leave it open!' he called, thwarting Jess again. With it open, he was better able to see the front door should she try to leave.

She had to find another way.

◆ ◆ ◆

It wasn't until the early hours of the following morning that Jess finally tried to run away. Her father, and then her mother upon her return from work, had kept such a close eye on her all day that there had simply been no earlier opportunity. They had both stayed up later than usual, and several times she had caught one or the other of them looking in on her as she pretended to sleep.

But they themselves had to sleep sometime.

Jess thought it was around three in the morning when at last she slipped out of bed, being extra careful not to disturb Hannah beside her. First she listened. She could hear her mother snoring in the other room, tired out from her long hours at the match works, and from being kept up late by Harry, whom she thought was no doubt counting in his sleep the minutes before Mr Butterfill would return with the agreed payment. Jess could not hear him, and that troubled her because he always snored. Still, she supposed that even he, who did so little all day to tire himself, had to be asleep by now, so she dressed quietly, knelt down and tied her boots, then crept out on to the landing, cringing with every step lest the boards beneath her creaked too loudly.

She made it all the way to the bottom of the stairs before one did. She instantly picked her foot up again and froze, listening, her heart pounding, expecting the worst. A moment later she heard her father and her heart began to beat faster still. He had not gone up to bed at all. He was still in the downstairs front room. She heard him stir, and then she heard him snort a few times before he settled again. Very slowly, she went to the front-room door and looked in. He had moved his armchair closer to the door, facing it so that he would be able to see if she tried to steal away in the night – if he had been able to keep awake. She saw an empty gin bottle lying on the floor beside him and thought his choice of company that night a poor one under the circumstances, but that was all the better for her.

Confident now that it would take more than a creaking floorboard to disturb him, Jess went into the scullery and collected the apron she had throughout the day filled with provisions. She wrapped it into a bundle, tied the strings around it, and then tiptoed up to the front door, where she very gently lifted the catch. She took a quick glance through the front-room doorway at her father again before she opened it. He still looked dead to the world, so without another moment's delay, she stepped out into the lamplit street and very slowly, very quietly, pulled the door to behind her.

'Come here!'

It was her father. Before Jess could fully shut the door, it shot violently open.

'Where do you think you're off to?' Harry yelled, grabbing at Jess as he came out into the street after her.

Jess gave a startled gasp, but her fear of him did not root her to the spot, as it might once have done. Now, she had resolve on her side, and her freedom ahead of her – freedom from him and the life she no longer cared for. Above all, she wanted freedom from Mr Butterfill. As she turned to run, however, she felt her father's hand grab at her hair. Her neck jerked back and she was forced to stop, but she would not give up so easily. She turned to face him, and with all her strength she drove the toe of her boot into his shin. Perhaps he did have a bad leg after all, because he immediately let go of her hair and began to hop on the spot, clutching his shin with both hands and crying out with pain. When he tried to grab her again, he was too late. She was running.

'You ungrateful little wretch!' Her father shouted after her. 'What about your little brother and your sisters? What about me?'

Jess turned to see him coming after her, but he was hopping and limping so much that he quickly fell behind. She ran and she ran, turning down one dark street after another until she could no longer hear him and everything around her seemed new and unfamiliar. She slowed, suddenly feeling hot from her exertion and the night air, which was surprisingly warm and humid. She began to walk, but she still kept up a brisk pace, taking in everything around her as she went. Had she been here before? She hadn't run that far. At least, it hadn't felt as if she had. Perhaps it all seemed so new to her because it was night-time and she never went out at night. She thought the shadows the gas lamps cast made everything seem so different.

She turned another corner and saw a pub she had never heard of, but she thought that was perhaps not so unlikely as there were so many in the area around Pottery Lane. Her eyes were drawn to the lamp that was still lit in the window, even at this hour. She picked up her pace again as she passed by, looking up at the sky for any signs of daybreak. There were none. The night was as black as the toes of her boots. When she looked down at the street again, she saw several people lying on the pavement ahead of her, sleeping in what appeared to be piles of old rags. She crossed the road, mindful of the horse dung, hoping her siblings would not soon share the same fate on account of her actions.

Further along, the silhouette of a bottle kiln stood out among the houses. There were many of them in the Potteries, and it gave her no further clue as to precisely where she was. She gravitated towards it, wondering whether it was still in use, and if it might offer her refuge off the streets until daybreak. She had heard such terrible stories about the things that went on in Notting Dale after dark, and with every passing minute she felt more and more vulnerable. She had food with her, after all. Who among those she met would think twice about slitting her throat for it?

Her imagination began to run away with her. Then she saw someone walking towards her on the opposite side of the street – a shadowy figure that she could barely make out in the gloom. He cocked his head towards her as they passed, and she looked down at her feet, wondering what business he was about at that hour, just as he was no doubt curious as to hers. Not for the first time that night, Jess's heart began to pound. What was she doing? Where did she intend to go anyway? She had made no plans beyond running away from her father and Mr Butterfill. Which street should she take next? She had no idea.

'Need some help, do you?'

A man stepped out from the shadows so abruptly that Jess caught her breath. She stopped instantly, too scared to answer.

'Now, don't be afraid,' he said, clearly noticing the fear in Jess's eyes. 'I only want to help. Lost, are you?'

Jess shook her head, lying, but she didn't want this man, whoever he was, to think her more vulnerable than she already knew she was.

'Late for a stroll, though, ain't it?' he said, stepping closer.

She heard another voice then. This time it came from behind her. 'What you got in your bundle there?'

She turned, and found herself caught between the two men. They had clearly seen her coming, even if she had not seen them.

'I think we'd best get you and your bundle off the streets,' the first man said.

'Yeah, it's no place for a young lady like yourself,' the other man said.

Then both men grabbed her tightly by her arms.

CHAPTER NINE

Present day

Black's Fine Art Prints was one of a parade of shops on Kennington Road, just south of Lambeth North Tube station. It was another warm spring afternoon, and as the address Nat had found on the Companies House website wasn't far from the Marcus Brown School of Family History, where Tayte and Nat had agreed to meet that afternoon, they walked there. Along the way they talked about Jess, as they imagined the kind of life she might have led as a child growing up on the streets of North Kensington in the late 1800s, about Nat's stolen painting, and about the eldest of the artist's direct living descendants, Brendan Black, whom Tayte hoped they were about to meet.

The fine art prints shop was sandwiched between a supermarket and a tattoo parlour. When Tayte and Nat arrived outside, Tayte's immediate thought was that the word 'Fine' on the shop's name above the door was at odds with the general tattiness of the facade. They stood at the display window for a moment, taking the place in. The paint was dirty and peeling, the glass covered in road-traffic film, and the display itself looked as if it hadn't been refreshed in years. There were a few prints with curled edges and faded borders on an assortment of wooden and dull brass easels, a jar, replete with dusty paintbrushes, and for reasons Tayte could not fathom, an inflatable red, white and blue beach ball that was as deflated as Tayte was beginning to feel just standing there, observing what amounted to obvious neglect. It was May, and yet he could even see some old magenta tinsel left over from a Christmas past.

He turned to Nat and gave her a knowing look. 'I'd say this place explains the company's balance sheet perfectly,' he said. He opened the door, inviting Nat to go inside. 'Shall we?'

Inside the shop, the ageing decor offered no further encouragement. There were several wire carousels dotted here and there, containing small, postcard-sized prints. Wooden bins lined the walls to either side, holding some of the larger prints on offer, inviting would-be browsers to thumb through them in search of something they liked. On the walls, Tayte saw such a random assortment of framed images that it suggested they had been placed there with little consideration. Only half of the spotlights illuminating them worked.

At the far end of the deep but narrow shop floor was a counter, and behind that counter, with an old-style green telephone handset pressed to his ear, was the man, Tayte presumed, he and Nat had gone there to see. The man muttered something into the telephone mouthpiece and hung up the call as soon as he saw them.

'Good afternoon to you,' he said as he came out from behind the counter. He was a short, slim man in his late fifties, dressed in a grey pinstripe three-piece suit. His fingers dripped with chunky gold rings. 'That's a lovely print, isn't it?' he added, indicating a print on the wall to

Tayte's left. 'Wonderful colours.'

Tayte hadn't really noticed it, having given the entire wall no more than a cursory glance.

'I can do you a special deal on that if you're interested,' the man continued. He came closer, pushing the knot of his mauve silk tie further up into his neck as he walked.

'Thank you,' Tayte said, being polite, 'but we're not here to buy anything.'

'Don't be so sure about that,' the man said, a cheesy smile on his face. 'Wait 'til you've had a gander through these prints over here,' he added, waving a hand towards the bins on his left.

'Perhaps later,' Tayte said. 'First, we'd like to talk to you about your artist ancestor, Stephen Ebenezer Black. You are Brendan Black?'

'I am,' Brendan said, his smile suddenly gone. It was replaced by a suspicious squint. He looked at Nat, then back at Tayte, taking them both in more fully, as if seeing them in a different light now from when they first walked in as prospective customers. 'What about him?'

'I'm a genealogist,' Tayte said. 'I teach family history.' He gestured to Nat. 'This is one of my students.'

Nat offered Brendan a smile. 'One of your ancestor's paintings has been in my family for decades,' she said. 'A portrait of a girl called Jess. We're trying to find out more about her.'

'Jess?' Brendan repeated, the set of his brow deepening further.

'That's right,' Tayte said. 'Have you heard the name before, perhaps in connection with one of your ancestor's paintings?'

'No,' Brendan said. 'Look, how did you know where to

find me?'

It didn't feel right to Tayte to say that they had gone digging into his business information at Companies House, publicly available as it was, so before Nat could answer he said, 'We went to see an art expert yesterday at Tate Britain. He showed us one of your ancestor's paintings and told us your father bequeathed it to the gallery, and thusly to the nation. He mentioned that you and your family continue to run your late father's fine art prints business.'

'Did he indeed?' Brendan said. He seemed put out at knowing someone had been talking about him. He scoffed. 'Well, he got part of it right. I continue to run the business, but my brothers and my sister never wanted anything to do with it.'

'So Felicity Greenwood is your sister?' Nat said.

'That's right,' Brendan said, clarifying that the only non-Black surname Tayte and Nat had seen on the Companies House register was also one of the family, as they had suspected. 'Each of them holds a share in the business, for what it's worth, as was our father's wish, but they're a part of it in name only, if you catch my drift.'

'Sleeping partners,' Tayte said.

'Exactly. We don't see much of each other, and that's fine by me. A card at Christmas is about it these days. What else did this art expert tell you?'

The phone behind the shop counter began to ring, but Brendan made no attempt to answer it.

'Do you want to get that?' Tayte asked. 'We're in no hurry.' He might have thought the business had a lucrative telesales revenue stream coming in, if he didn't already know better from the company's recent filing history.

'It can wait,' Brendan said. 'Go on.'

Nat answered. 'He said you thought your father's painting should have gone to you,' she said, 'and that it was the last of S E Black's works held by the family. Is that true?'

The phone stopped ringing and Brendan huffed. 'Unfortunately it is,' he said. 'And yes, that painting bloody well should have come to me. I'm the eldest, after all, and as I've said, I'm the only one who's ever taken any interest in this place. My father owed me that painting.'

Brendan's sour expression told Tayte that he was still upset by his father's decision, and subsequently the court's, to leave the painting in the care of Tate Britain, so he thought it best to steer the conversation back to the primary reason he and Nat were there.

'Do you know if your artist ancestor, Stephen Black, catalogued his work?' he asked, thinking that might be the only way anyone could know about the portrait of Jess today.

'Possibly,' Brendan said.

'Did your father leave anything to you or your siblings by way of records from that time?' Tayte asked, thinking it would be good to see them if he did. Maybe there would be something that connected Jess to the artist or his family.

Brendan nodded. 'There were some old papers in a trunk in the attic.'

Tayte and Nat exchanged smiles.

'I don't have anything, though,' Brendan continued, dashing Tayte's hopes. 'My sister took the house on, after buying the rest of us out, of course. Maybe she has something.' He took a step towards the bins he'd previously indicated, against the wall to his left. 'Now, I think I've been as helpful as I can.'

'Yes, of course,' Tayte said. 'Thanks for talking to us.' He reached into his jacket pocket and pulled out a business card, which he handed to Brendan. 'Perhaps you'd call me if the name Jess conjures up any memories,' he added, and then he and Nat turned to leave.

'Hold on a minute!' Brendan said. 'You're going to buy something before you go, aren't you?'

'Excuse me?' Tayte said, turning back.

Brendan gestured to the art bins. 'Seems only fair,' he said. 'At least come and take a look – see if something takes your fancy.'

Tayte hid his sigh well enough that only Nat could hear it. As they followed Brendan to the art bins, he thought information at a price was indeed fair enough in his game, and it was certainly nothing new to him.

CHAPTER TEN

Tayte parted company with Nat outside Lambeth North Tube station. She went home to Spitalfields, north of the Thames, and he walked the short distance back to the Marcus Brown School of Family History to set up for his Friday evening class. It was barely five o'clock. He had plenty of time, so he took a casual stroll, letting his thoughts wander, eager now to go and see Brendan Black's siblings, which he'd agreed with Nat they would try to do the following afternoon. He had his briefcase in one hand, and in the other, tucked beneath his arm, was the fine art print he'd just been cajoled into buying.

Thankfully, he'd found something that appealed to his love of musicals: a small print of an old *Playbill* magazine cover from the 1950s that featured a scene from *West Side Story*. It depicted Maria in the foreground, pulling Tony along behind her as they ran through the streets of New York's Upper West Side, their faces full of smiles. Tayte wasn't sure it qualified as fine art, but as he'd felt obliged to buy something from the shop's proprietor for taking the time to talk to him and Nat, he was glad to have found something he liked.

He turned a corner and his eyes fell on the building he was heading for, all the while trying to protect his cellophane-wrapped print from all the people hurrying past him and into him, the evening rush hour in full flow around him. When he drew closer to the entrance, he saw a smartly dressed woman in a bright-green dress, standing alongside two casually dressed men in jeans and polo shirts. One of them had a camera perched on his shoulder, the other a fluffy boom microphone on a long pole. When Tayte passed their television news van and realised who they were, he wondered what the attraction was. Only when he reached them and paused to polish the plaque outside the school with the sleeve of his jacket did he realise that the news reporter and her crew were there for him.

'Excuse me,' the reporter said. 'Are you Jefferson Tayte?'

Tayte turned around, surprised to hear his name. 'I am,' he said, a puzzled look on his face. It wasn't the first time he'd been in the news because of an assignment he was working on, but he was teaching now, just trying to help a young woman discover more about someone in her family tree. That was the line he kept selling himself, but deep down he was fully aware of the terrible crime at the heart of it all. Just the same, he wondered how the assignment could have caught the attention of the media so soon. How did they even know who he was, let alone what he was working on?

The female reporter came towards him, pushing her short blonde hair back over one ear as she approached. The camera and the boom microphone quickly followed her. 'I'm Zoe Young for KMI London News,' she said into her own small microphone. 'Do you mind if I ask you a few questions about the painting you discovered?'

Tayte just wanted to go up to his classroom and munch on a few Hershey's Miniatures while he went over the evening's subject matter, but he didn't want to be rude, and he was slightly put out by the suggestion that he had discovered the painting.

'It wasn't my discovery,' he said. 'The painting belongs to a young woman who may or may not be related to the subject. She came to me hoping to prove the connection and find out more about her.'

'I see,' the reporter said, 'and in doing so you've learned that the painting is a hitherto unknown work by the artist S E Black, worth in excess of two million pounds.'

Tayte laughed. 'I don't know where you got that number from, but—' He stopped himself. Of course he knew. It had to have come from the art expert, Barrett Huckabee. He was the reason the news reporter was there. Tayte figured he must have gone to the press about the discovery soon after he and Nat left him the day before. 'Two million pounds?' he repeated, almost to himself, as the number sank in.

'That is the auction estimate given to us by a reliable source,' the reporter said. 'We've also been told that the painting was recently stolen, and that it may be connected with the murder of one of the victim's relatives the very same week. Can you confirm that?'

'Yes,' Tayte said, thinking it no wonder that whoever stole it had gone to the lengths they had to track it down, and along the way had even been prepared to kill for it.

The news crew seemed to crowd Tayte now as they all moved closer. 'Have you spoken with the police?' the reporter asked. 'Do they have any idea who may have stolen the painting?'

'I've not spoken with them personally, no,' Tayte said. 'The woman the painting belongs to has. As far as I know they have no leads at this time.'

'And do you believe that your work in the field of genealogy could help them with their investigation? Could it lead to the painting's recovery?'

'I don't know,' Tayte said. His work had helped the police many times before, but on this occasion he thought it was too soon to form any opinion on the matter. Maybe one of S E Black's descendants was behind this, maybe not. He had to remind himself, though, that they were perhaps best placed to know that the formerly unknown painting of Jess existed. He just intended to keep digging and see what crawled out of the woodwork. 'If you'll excuse me,' he added, 'I have a class to prepare for.' He turned to go, but the reporter continued with her questions.

'You're no stranger to helping the police solve some of their more complex cases, are you?' she called after him. 'You've worked with the Devon and Cornwall Police and the Kent Police, to name just a couple. You've even helped the Security Service with matters of national security. Mr Tayte, you're clearly good at what you do. Surely you have high hopes of bringing this thief, and murderer, to justice?'

Tayte paused. This news team had certainly done their homework on him, but he wouldn't be drawn. 'No comment,' he said as he stepped inside the building and closed the door.

CHAPTER ELEVEN

North Kensington, London
1891

'Leave her be, the pair of you!'

Jess had barely had time to struggle against the two men who had grabbed her, on whichever dark street she had happened upon when she ran away from home, when she saw a woman crossing the road. The woman strode confidently towards them, elbows flared, her squat top hat wobbling from side to side, setting the feather atop it dancing as she walked.

'I said, leave her be!' she repeated when she reached them, her tone as fiery as her temper seemed to be. 'Will you both be deaf now, as well as daft?'

Jess felt the pressure on her arms ease a little. She thought the overly made-up woman, whose cheeks were as red as the tatty velvet dress she was wearing, had a peculiar accent. It reminded her of the Irishman and his family who had briefly lived a few doors down from her and her family a year or so ago. There was no question in her mind that the woman was a prostitute, but whoever she was, and whatever her business at this hour, she was glad to see her.

'Calm down now, Maggie, won't you?' one of the men

said. 'We was just having a bit of fun to pass the night.'

'Yeah, calm down,' the other man chipped in. 'You'll have the whole street awake in a minute.'

'So take your hands off the poor girl, and be away with you,' Maggie said. 'Or I'll have everyone hanging out of their windows to see what you're up to!'

'All right, all right,' the first man said, letting go of Jess as he put both his hands up as if in surrender. 'We're going.'

The other man let go of Jess, too, but as he did so, he leaned in and tried to kiss her. Maggie responded on her behalf more quickly than Jess was able to. From her belt, she pulled out something that Jess thought looked like a riding crop and slapped it down across the back of the man's neck.

'We'll be having none of that, now,' she said, giving him a disdainful glare.

The man winced from the blow. Then he also put his hands up. 'Another time then, Maggie,' he said, rubbing at his neck.

'Not too soon, I hope,' Maggie retorted as they headed off along the street with their tails between their legs.

As soon as they were lost to the darkness, Jess looked up at Maggie and offered her a smile. 'Thank you,' she said. 'That was very brave of you.'

'Brave?' Maggie repeated, almost laughing. 'What, against that pair of eejits?'

'You know them?'

Maggie nodded. 'More's the pity. I know most around here who like to stay out after dark, but I don't know you, now, do I?'

Jess shook her head. 'I'm Jessie,' she said. 'People call me Jess.'

Maggie pulled Jess's hand up from her side and gently shook it. 'In that case, I'm Margaret, but, as you've heard, people call me Maggie. I'm pleased to meet you.'

Jess laughed. Maybe it was Maggie's accent, or the relief of having been rescued, but in her company Jess suddenly felt safe again.

'New to all this, are you?' Maggie asked.

Jess pulled a face. 'New to what?'

'Being out on the streets at night, of course.'

'Oh,' Jess said. 'Yes, it's the first time I've been out at night by myself.'

'Well now, you'll be needing a prettier dress than that for sure,' Maggie said, 'and I'd team up with someone if I were you.' She laughed to herself. 'It's all right for a seasoned old whore like me to be going it alone, but there's safety in numbers, at least until you learn the ropes. I'd finish earlier, too, if I were you.'

It took a while for Jess to twig what Maggie meant. She felt her cheeks flush. 'You've got it wrong,' she said. 'I ain't a...' She trailed off, looking for the right word – one she didn't mind saying, and that wouldn't offend.

'You're not a whore, is that it?'

Jess shook her head quite fiercely. 'No, miss, I ain't.'

Maggie threw her head back and laughed out loud. 'I'm just messing with you. Any fool could see you're not. But tell me, why then are you out on the streets at this hour, and for the first time, you say?'

'I'm running away from home.'

'Are you now? And where exactly is home?'

Jess did not want to tell her in case she insisted on dragging her back there, whether she felt it was for her own good or not.

'You don't have to tell me,' Maggie said a few moments later, sensing her hesitation. 'I ran away from home, too, when I was about your age. Our reasons are our own, are they not?'

Jess relaxed again. She nodded.

'Do you know where it is you're going?' Maggie asked.

'Not really, no.'

Maggie drew a long, thoughtful breath. 'No, I didn't, either. Still, you don't want to be staying around here. I'd head south, if I were you. I find the people are much nicer there.'

Jess looked around her, wondering which way that was.

Maggie laughed again. 'I'll walk with you a while,' she said. 'It's nearly daybreak. I'll stick with you until then. Would you like that?'

'Yes, please,' Jess said. 'I'd like that very much.'

Maggie's next kindly gesture felt strange to Jess, not least because it was something her mother had never done. She took Jess's hand in hers, holding it tightly, reassuringly, and together they headed off along the street.

'Come along with you, then,' Maggie said. 'If we step it out, we should reach Kensington Gardens in time to hear the first robin sing.'

CHAPTER TWELVE

By daybreak, Jess was standing by a tall iron railing, looking into Kensington Gardens. The royal park was not quite open yet, but as Maggie had said, 'It makes no difference anyways. The likes of us aren't welcome in there – least, not unless we're in our Sunday best.' Apart from her boots, Jess didn't have a 'Sunday best', but she could at least have a look. Peering in, she thought it was the most peaceful, calming place at this early hour that she had ever known. Birdsong filled the air. In the trees, squirrels darted and chattered, and on the lake Maggie had told her about, she imagined that the ducks and the swans were stirring.

'Good luck to you,' Maggie had said as she left, and Jess had not wanted to let go of her hand.

She tilted her head back and was in awe of the sunrise. It was all encompassing, as red as a blood orange, lighting up the sky as if it were on fire. She wondered what the new day had in store for her – her first day of freedom – and she was not afraid of it. She let out a contented sigh as she returned to watching the birds in their merry flight. Time passed without her awareness, until the sky was not red but blue as a cornflower. A few pigeons began to gather at her feet, and she dipped into her little bundle. She pulled out her heel of bread and tore off a piece for them, though she knew she could not really spare it. As she broke it into crumbs, she was, for a brief moment at least, without a care.

Once the hypnotic effect of the park's beauty began to wear off, however, her thoughts turned to what she was going to do with her new-found freedom. The city streets were quickly coming to life around her, drowning out the birdsong. She looked away from the park at last and considered which way to go. South, in the direction she had been heading, seemed the obvious choice as she did not want to risk winding up back where she'd started, so she set off towards a pretty tree-lined avenue she could see. She figured she had all day to decide what she was going to do, but right now she wanted to find somewhere peaceful, like the park, where she would be able to stop and rest and eat something, away from the fast-growing number of people and the traffic. Feeding the pigeons had made her stomach groan.

The pretty avenue she had seen turned into an even prettier square when she was partway along it. Grand, white-painted Georgian houses lined the square on all sides in regimented terraces, each set back from the pavement across lawns that were twenty or so feet deep. In the middle of the square, behind more iron railings, was a gated garden full of benches and roses and other flora. She went up to the gate, thinking how lovely it would be to eat her breakfast, for what it was, on one of the benches, but to her disappointment, it was also locked. Turning away, however, she saw what she thought was the next best thing. Across the street, at the end of a pathway that ran up to one of the houses, was a low wall and gate, and a gleaming white step. It drew her eye, and not to be disheartened she went to it, thinking she could sit there instead. It was a peaceful spot, after all, and she could see most of the flower garden across from her.

As she sat down, she set her little bundle of provisions on her lap and began to untie it, wondering what she should eat first. Potato peel was not as appealing as bread and dripping, but once that was gone it was gone, and she thought it would be nice to still have it to look forward to, so she took out a piece of potato peel. It was full of goodness, her mother had once told her, while she was showing her how to make a potato peel pie. She took a small bite to make it last, and as she did so, she caught the most heavenly smell. It was not the limp piece of potato peel in her hand, but that of freshly baked bread.

Jess's stomach groaned so loudly that it would have drawn the attention of anyone passing by, had there been anyone there to hear it. She swivelled around, craning her head back towards the tall, broad-fronted house she was sitting outside. Some of the windows were open. She could only imagine that the wonderful aroma had wafted through the entire house from the kitchen. She suddenly lost interest in her greying piece of potato peel. Retying her bundle, she stood up. What she wouldn't give for a piece of that freshly baked bread. Her mouth began to water. She knew she had to go up to the house and ask for some – just a small piece. What harm was there in that? She had been sent out to beg before, and this was not so different, surely?

She tried the low gate and silently it swung open on well-oiled hinges. She took two steps along the path, hesitating only momentarily before she took another two, and then another. She was halfway to the front door by now, but then she paused. She heard voices behind her and saw two gentlemen in fine black suits and top hats coming along the pavement, heavily engaged in conversation. She thought little of it at first, so she continued almost all of the way to the house. The aromas of baked bread grew stronger with every step. She was almost there, but then to her horror the front door began to open. Behind her, the gentlemen she had seen had paused by the gate, although thankfully they did not look at her once as they continued to discuss whatever it was that so preoccupied them.

Jess lost her nerve that instant. There was no question in her mind that the two gentlemen were visiting the house. Now, someone had come to the front door to let them in. There were tall, ornamental trees in lead containers to either side of the entrance. She darted across to the tree on her right as the door fully opened, concealing herself as best she could behind it as a woman dressed all in black – the housekeeper, Jess supposed – came out and walked down the path to greet the visitors. Jess felt her breath quicken. What was she to do? If she stayed where she was, she would surely be seen as soon as the housekeeper turned around, but she could hardly reveal herself now without causing a stir. She half expected that if she did, she would be up before the magistrate by the time the day was out. She had to find somewhere else to hide until they were all inside.

Stepping out on to the path again, crouching as low as she could while keeping the housekeeper between her and the two gentlemen, Jess was all too aware that there was nowhere else to hide. The house had such a tidy frontage that the small trees to either side of the entrance were her only cover. She heard the housekeeper greet the gentlemen and knew she was out of time. Frantically, she looked to her left and to her right, trying to decide which way to run. The housekeeper began to turn around and Jess felt close to panic. Then, without thinking, she saw the front door, half open as the housekeeper had left it, and she dashed into the house, her heart pounding as she pushed the door to behind her.

◆ ◆ ◆

Inside the house, Jess found herself standing in a deep entrance hall, looking at several closed doors and a staircase, wondering which way to go. Her instinct was to get as far away from the front door as possible, before the housekeeper came back with the two gentlemen she had gone out to greet, so she ran past the staircase as quietly as she could, over a black-and-white chequered floor, to the back of the hall. She had to find somewhere to hide until she could leave the house unseen. She saw that one of the doors here was ajar. She went to it, and just as the front door opened and the housekeeper stepped into the house with the two gentlemen, she ducked inside, panting heavily as she leaned her back against it, closing it with a barely audible click.

When Jess took stock of where she was, she found herself in what appeared to be a library of sorts. She couldn't be quite sure, because while there were a lot of books stacked all around her on floor-to-ceiling mahogany shelves, there was also a good deal of brass apparatus here and there. It suggested that the room had another purpose. She moved further in, trying to decide what that purpose could be. The ceiling was very high, and there was a spiral staircase at the far end of the room, which led up to a mezzanine level and a galleried iron walkway that wrapped around the room to facilitate access to the books on the upper shelves. In the middle of the room was the largest of the apparatus, and above it a domed glass cupola through which the early morning sunlight lit up the room.

Jess was fascinated by it. The bevelled, prismatic edges of the glass panels filled the room with beautiful patterns in all colours of the spectrum. She gravitated towards the central apparatus, all the while looking up into the light as if mesmerised by it, her mind questioning where all these multicoloured lights were coming from. Not paying attention to where she was walking, she bumped into the central apparatus and took it in more fully. It comprised a long brass tube the diameter of a side plate, mounted to a wooden base that was bolted to the floor. It had large cogged wheels attached to it, with handles to turn them, which she supposed were used to rotate and reposition the brass tube. She had no idea what it was.

She went to the desk next and found other, smaller apparatus there, some in felt-lined wooden cases, others just laid out on the desk. She picked up one of the objects and ran her fingers over the cool brass-work. She thought it looked a lot like a sundial, but it had little stars engraved on it and letters around the outside that she quickly realised represented the months of the year.

'Stars,' she said under her breath, beginning to understand now what else this room was used for.

She thought one of the books might confirm it, so she took one out and thumbed through it, looking for drawings, but it was mostly just a lot of words, and what pictures she did see were of things she could not understand. She closed it again. It was all very interesting, but she knew it was time to go. She thought she had spent too long there already, and the housekeeper was sure to have moved on with the two visitors by now. She was about to return the book to its place on the shelf and make her exit, but just as she raised the book, she stopped cold as something above her creaked. It reminded her of the sound her father's old leather chair made on the seldom occasion that he ever got out of it. She looked up, and standing before a tall wing-back chair, also with a book in his hand, was a short, well-fed man in a plain grey suit. He wore a colourful red bow tie at his neck, and a quizzical expression on his face.

'And who might you be?' he asked as he began to descend the spiral staircase to find out.

CHAPTER THIRTEEN

Present day

Jefferson Tayte's Saturday morning class on immigration records finished a little after midday. As soon as he'd said goodbye to the seven students who had attended, he sat back in his chair, opened his briefcase, and pulled out his lunch. As it was Saturday, instead of his usual lettuce and tomato sandwiches, he was having sushi, courtesy of the takeaway restaurant he'd passed on his way there – having ridden his bicycle more than a little out of his way to pass it. He broke the included wooden chopsticks apart and picked up a piece of ebi-nigiri, thinking about Nat, who was meeting him there at one o'clock, and about their chances of talking to the rest of the Black family that afternoon. He dunked the prawn side of the nigiri into his little pot of soy sauce, and he was about to put it into his mouth when a man appeared in the doorway at the far end of the room, filling the frame.

'Mr Jefferson Tayte?' the man enquired as he knocked on the open door.

His mouth by now watering, Tayte reluctantly put his sushi down. 'Yes,' he said, as he wondered who the man was. He had the feeling he wasn't there to enquire about attending one of his classes. Maybe it was the dark suit and tie on a Saturday, or the official tone in his voice. The man approached. He was tall and black skinned, with a bald head and short, wiry grey stubble on his face. As he came closer, he seemed larger than life to Tayte, as if he'd just stepped out of the pages of a Marvel comic. He had a muscular physique, arms bulging in his jacket sleeves. Unlike Tayte, his lumps were in all the right places.

'My apologies,' he said, noticing Tayte's sushi on the desk. 'I didn't mean to interrupt your lunch.'

Tayte detected an East London accent, but it seemed somehow refined at the same time. 'I hadn't really started it yet,' he said, smiling. 'How can I help you?'

'My name's Dalton,' the man said. 'Detective Inspector Dalton.'

'Then I'm guessing you're here about the painting?'

'And a murder,' Dalton said.

'Yes, of course,' Tayte said, getting to his feet. 'Let me grab you a chair.'

Tayte hadn't tidied anything away yet. The folding chairs were all still out at their desks. As he came around from behind his desk to fetch a chair for Dalton, Dalton put up a hand up to stop him.

'There's no need,' he said. 'I prefer to stand, if you don't mind. I won't take too much of your time – let you get back to your lunch.'

Tayte did not prefer to stand, so he sat down again.

'Is that wasabi?' Dalton asked, eyeing the green paste through a grimace.

'Yes, it is. You want some?'

Dalton shook his head vigorously. 'Can't stand the stuff,' he said. 'Tried it once – nearly blew my socks off. I saw you on the local news last night.'

Tayte had already figured as much, and he wasn't surprised to know that news of the painting's value, and perhaps of his involvement, had rekindled police interest in the case. 'I'm afraid I can't really tell you any more than I told the news reporter.'

'Perhaps not yet,' Dalton said. 'But in time, who knows? You said you were helping the owner of the painting, a Miss Natalie Cooper, to find out more about the subject of the painting.'

'That's correct,' Tayte said. 'We're in the process of talking to the artist's descendants now.'

'Are you?' Dalton said, raising his eyebrows with interest.

It made Tayte wonder whether the police were also interested in the artist's descendants. 'We'd like to know what became of the painting's subject, a young girl from the late 1800s called Jessie Bates.'

'I see,' Dalton said. He paused, rubbing at the stubble on his chin. 'I've not had the time to look into it,' he said a moment later, 'but last night the reporter also said that your specialist skills had been of help to the police before. Is that right?'

The question forced Tayte to think back over some of those occasions, many of which he would sooner forget. 'Many times,' he said, his tone heavier than he'd intended. 'Over the years I've learned that clues and connections to people and their crimes can often be found in the records they leave behind. It's just a matter of knowing where to look for them, and how to piece the puzzle together so you can see the bigger picture.'

Dalton nodded. 'I think you may be able to help me,' he said. 'You told the reporter you didn't know whether your work could lead to the painting's recovery, but between you and me, what's your gut instinct on this?'

'My instinct,' Tayte said, 'tells me that someone in the artist's family knows something about the theft of the painting. It's a hitherto unknown portrait, which in itself is quite unusual for this particular artist. A single family has owned it for several decades, and they didn't even know what it was. I struggle to see who else could know of its existence.'

'I like the way your mind works, Mr Tayte,' Dalton said. 'That's a very good point. So, you believe someone in the artist's family stole the painting?'

'I didn't say that.'

'No, but you could well be right. Just as killers are often known to their victims, so are a great many other types of criminal connected in some way to the victims of their crimes. It seems that we're both in the business of exploiting those connections to reach our goals, aren't we?'

'I guess we are,' Tayte said.

'This is a murder investigation now, of course,' Dalton continued. 'Given the estimated value of the painting, there's no doubt that's what the killer was after. I don't think he meant to kill Miss Cooper's cousin, but murder is murder. I want to find him, Mr Tayte, and by any means available to me.'

'Of course,' Tayte said, fully understanding what Dalton meant. 'And by *any means available* I take it you mean me?'

'I do,' Dalton said. 'If you can, I'd like you to help me bring this killer to justice.'

Tayte drew a long, deep breath. While he was under no illusion that this was just another genealogical brick wall he was helping someone with, having known all along that Nat wanted him to help her to find her cousin's killer, hearing Inspector Dalton say it made it all the more official.

'I could go and talk to them,' Dalton continued, as if sensing Tayte's hesitancy, 'but it would be on shaky grounds at this point in the investigation, and people are often less relaxed when they know they're talking to the police. Someone like yourself, on the other hand, talking about family history, could hear something a policeman might not, if you catch my drift.'

Tayte nodded. 'I understand, Inspector,' he said. 'And yes, of course, I'd be happy to help with your investigation in any way I can.'

Dalton smiled. It was the first Tayte had seen.

'Great,' Dalton said. He reached into his jacket and gave Tayte his card. 'If you hear anything you believe might be of value to the investigation, call this number. Likewise if you need help with anything. You're not to put yourself or anyone around you in danger, is that understood?'

'Perfectly,' Tayte said. He'd received that part loud and clear. 'I'm a teacher now,' he added, almost to himself, as if to suggest that he'd left all that in the past.

'Good,' Dalton said, reaching a hand across the desk.

Tayte's hands were big and strong by any standard, but he winced a little when Dalton grabbed one of them and shook it. Tayte smiled to cover it up, already thinking about his now official role in yet another murder investigation. But he was only doing what he usually did, he told himself. He was just talking to the family. What harm could possibly come of that? He stopped himself. He'd thought that before, and on more than one occasion it had very nearly killed him. As Inspector Dalton made for the door, Tayte reminded himself that anyone who had committed murder, whether intentionally or otherwise, might not hesitate to do so again.

CHAPTER FOURTEEN

South Kensington, London
1891

Having been discovered by the man in the plain grey suit, Jess's first instinct was to run. She did not think he would take kindly to finding her in his library, or whatever it was, so as the man continued down the spiral staircase to confront her, she made for the door.

'Wait!' the man called. 'I won't harm you. You're in no trouble.'

Jess paused, her hand on the doorknob, wondering whether or not to believe him. She turned around to face him. He was at the foot of the staircase now, smiling at her. He made no effort to come closer.

'Who are you?' he asked. 'Whatever brings you here?'

Jess thought they were both very reasonable questions under the circumstances. 'I'm called Jess,' she said, thinking the man's round face looked kindly enough. She began to relax a little. She did not elaborate on why she was there.

A moment later, the man pointed to the book she was still holding. 'I see you have one of my books. Surely, that is not why you are here?'

Jess looked down at the book as if seeing it for the first time. In her eagerness to run out of the room, she had forgotten she still had it. 'No, 'course not,' she said, sounding offended by the suggestion.

'Then perhaps you would return it to me,' the man said, holding out his hand, still smiling warmly.

Jess narrowed her eyes at him.

He laughed. 'I have already told you, Jess. You have nothing to be afraid of here.' He took a step towards her and her hand tightened around the doorknob again. 'My name is Ephraim Black,' he added, taking another step, 'and you still have not told me how it is that you come to be here.'

Whether this Ephraim Black was kind or otherwise, Jess still wanted to run from there. Now, however, she could hear talking out in the hallway – the visitors, she supposed – so she thought she had no other choice than to accept this man's word. She let go of the doorknob and went to meet him, offering out the book as she did so. 'I was hungry,' she said. 'I smelled the bread baking. Heavenly it was, so I came to see if you could spare some. Then people came and I ran inside, all of a panic. You've got visitors, by the way.'

'Other than your good self?' Ephraim said. 'My, what an interesting start to the day. Well, I'm sure they can amuse themselves for a while longer. My housekeeper, Mrs Bramley, will no doubt take them into the drawing room and offer them a cup of tea before she comes to find me.' They were only a few steps away from one another now. Ephraim looked at the book Jess was holding out, his wiry grey eyebrows twitching. 'Now, what's this book that appears to have caught your interest?'

Jess stopped and looked at the cover. The only word she knew was Agnes, and that was only because she used to have a sister called Agnes, who died before her first birthday. She recognised the shapes of the letters from the little wreath of flowers someone had made. 'Don't know,' she said. 'I can't read, see.'

'Oh dear,' Ephraim said. 'Now that is perplexing.'

'Why's that?'

'Well, clearly you have taken a book down from one of my shelves in complete understanding of the fact that you would not be able to read it.'

'I wanted to look at the drawings.'

'Ah, I see. And why might that be?'

Jess waved her free hand around her at the apparatus. 'I thought they might tell me what all this stuff's for.'

'An inquisitive mind,' Ephraim said. 'I like that. And did you satisfy your curiosity?'

Jess shook her head. 'Not exactly. I couldn't understand the drawings, neither.'

Ephraim laughed. He leaned in and took the book from Jess, making no attempt to grab hold of her. '*A Popular History of Astronomy during the Nineteenth Century*,' he said, reading the book's title aloud. 'By Agnes Mary Clerke. It's a recent volume,' he added turning it in his hand, 'and a very good place to indulge one's interest in celestial studies and observations.'

'Celestial?' Jess said. 'Astronomy?' She had no idea what either word meant.

'The stars!' Ephraim said, spinning around as he looked up at the glass cupola above them.

'Oh,' Jess said, 'I thought that's what it was.'

'You did?' Ephraim said, his face full of enthusiasm.

Jess nodded. 'I saw some engraved on one of those

brass things there on the desk. The one that looks like a sundial.'

'That is called a nocturnal,' Ephraim said. 'It's very much like a sundial, but instead of telling the time from the position of the sun by day, it is used to tell the time from the relative positions of two or more stars by night.'

Jess wandered over to the large apparatus in the centre of the room beneath the cupola. 'Can you look at the stars through this brass tube?'

'Indeed I can,' Ephraim said, standing proudly beside her. 'This is my telescope. Above us, one of the glass panels opens up and the entire cupola can then be rotated, providing a window to the night sky. I then rotate this wheel,' he added, resting a hand on the largest of the cogged wheels before them, 'and by doing so I can align the telescope to the window, giving me a clear view of the heavens.'

There was a knock at the door and Ephraim tut-tutted. 'What a pity. That, no doubt, will be Mrs Bramley, and I was so enjoying myself. Come in!' he called.

The door opened and the woman Jess had seen on the path outside stepped in. She was about to speak, but when she saw Jess she stopped herself, a puzzled expression on her face. 'The two gentlemen you wished to see regarding Master Stephen's tutelage are here, sir,' she said a moment later, her eyes still on Jess. 'They're waiting for you in the drawing room.'

'Very good, Mrs Bramley,' Ephraim said. 'I'll be in to see them at once. Oh, this is Jess,' he added, clearly noticing Mrs Bramley's confusion. 'Would you take her to the kitchen to see Mrs Eady.' He turned to Jess and winked. 'I've promised her a good breakfast this morning.'

CHAPTER FIFTEEN

By the time Jess left Mrs Eady's kitchen, her stomach was feeling uncomfortably full. She had never seen so much good food, nor eaten so much in one sitting in all her life. The freshly baked bread had tasted even better than it had smelled, and she had been given meat, carved off the bone from a mouth-wateringly large leg of ham. She must have spent a good hour with Mrs Eady – who had insisted she call her Ann as soon as they met – before she decided it was time to be on her way lest she outstayed her welcome. Never fond of goodbyes with the people she liked, however, having thanked Ann with a big hug, she quietly slipped out of the kitchen while Ann had her back to her, rolling out pastry as she hummed a pleasant tune to herself. Jess thought she could find her own way back to the front door easily enough.

She was back in the entrance hall in no time, ambling across the black-and-white floor tiles, smiling contentedly to herself. She hadn't seen a soul since she left the kitchen, and it seemed unlikely to her now that she would, which she thought was a shame because she would have liked to thank her benefactor before she left. She had just arrived at the foot of the main staircase, wondering where Mr Black might be, when she heard what sounded like someone shouting. It was coming from one of the rooms at the top of the stairs. She listened more closely, but the sound had stopped. All she could hear now was the mellow tick-tock of the grandfather clock against the wall to her left. The sound she had taken for shouting was so fleeting that she quickly convinced herself she was mistaken, but as she continued towards the front door, she heard it again.

'Mr Black?' she called up. 'Is that you, sir?'

Jess took a couple of steps, peering up at the landing to see if anyone was there. She took a few more steps, listening for the sound again, but none came. It wasn't until her curiosity had taken her all the way to the top of the stairs that she heard it again. It was quieter this time, but clearly coming from the other side of the door immediately to her right. Now that she was so close, she thought that whoever was there sounded angry about something. A part of her wanted to run back down the stairs and leave at once, but if it was Mr Black, she still wanted to thank him, and he was not angry with her after all, so she knocked lightly and opened the door.

'Mr Black?' she said again as she poked her head inside the room.

What she saw, however, was not Ephraim Black, but a boy who looked a few years older than her, about the same height, with chestnut-brown hair and rosy, freckled cheeks. He was wearing green corduroy knickerbockers, and he had a brass tube in his hands that Jess thought looked similar to Mr Black's telescope, only much smaller.

'Who are you?' the boy asked, staring at her from a chair by the window.

Jess thought he looked far more angry over her intrusion than was called for, but she quickly realised it was not because of her sudden appearance, but that he was already angry at something before she opened the door. She wanted to close it again, but she thought that would be rude.

'Begging your pardon,' she said, taking this boy for the young Master Stephen she had previously heard the housekeeper mention. 'I'm Jess. I was just looking for your dad.'

'My father? Why?'

Jess opened the door more fully and stepped inside. 'He was kind to me. I wanted to thank him, that's all.'

'Well, he's not here, is he?' Stephen said, a little too curtly for Jess's liking. 'He's downstairs interviewing my new tutors.'

She noticed his cheeks redden further as he finished speaking. 'Is that why you're upset?' she asked. 'I heard you shouting.' She took in the room more fully, to be sure there were no other children hiding anywhere. The room was quite small and sparsely furnished with a small desk and a few more chairs here and there. They were quite alone. 'Was you just shouting at yourself, then?'

Stephen nodded, his cheeks still flushed, but now more from embarrassment, Jess thought.

'It's all right,' she said. 'I feel like doing that myself sometimes. Was it because of your new tutors? Don't you like being taught stuff?'

'Not by people I don't know,' Stephen said. 'I want my old tutors back, but my father said they weren't qualified to teach me. He said I needed special teachers.'

'Why's that then?'

Stephen began to fidget. He looked out of the window. 'I don't know. I get frustrated, I suppose, because I don't understand things as quickly as they expect me to.'

Jess went closer and Stephen gave no objection. 'Well, maybe these new teachers will help you understand better, so there won't be no need to get all frustrated. It probably won't be so bad once you get to know them. I mean, you didn't know me before I opened that door. Now we're getting along just fine, ain't we? You're not angry no more, are you?'

'Maybe just a bit,' Stephen said, looking at Jess again. He looked down into his lap, trying to hold back a smile.

Jess laughed. 'Told you so,' she said. 'You're not angry, and neither should you be. You're lucky is what you are. I'd love to be taught stuff, but my dad said as I was the eldest, I couldn't go to school 'cos I was needed at home to look after my little brother and sisters.' She went closer still, until she was standing right in front of him. 'What you got there, then?' she added, pointing to the brass tube he was holding in his lap.

Stephen turned it in his hands. 'It's called a kaleidoscope. You hold it up to the light and look into it. Then you turn—'

'I know what a kaleidoscope is,' Jess cut in. 'I seen plenty of people with them before. Not as fancy as that one, mind. Can I have a look?'

'It's rude to interrupt people when they're speaking,' Stephen said, lowering the kaleidoscope protectively back into his lap.

'My apologies, I'm sure,' Jess said, putting on a sarcastic voice. 'Now, can I have a look or not? I can just as well be on me way again.'

Stephen quickly offered up the kaleidoscope and Jess gave him a smile. 'Don't expect a penny for a peek like they do on the streets,' she said as she took it from him. 'That's not what friends do, and I ain't got no penny, neither.'

She turned to face the window, and was about to raise the kaleidoscope to her eye, expecting to see something quite magical through such a fine instrument, when there was a tap at the door and Ephraim Black walked in.

'Jess,' he said, surprised to see her there. He came into the room and closed the door behind him. 'I went to the kitchen to find you. I thought you must have already left.'

'Left?' Stephen said.

Jess gave him the kaleidoscope back. 'That's right,' she said. 'I must be going.'

'But you can't leave!'

'Stephen,' his father cut in. 'I'd like to introduce you to your new tutors. They're waiting in the drawing room and would like to come up and meet you before they go.'

Stephen glanced at Jess and she gave him a reassuring nod. 'All right,' he said.

'What's that?' Ephraim said, furrowing his brow. 'You don't mind? I expected you to throw one of your tantrums.' He looked at Jess, clearly having seen her nod. 'Do we somehow have you to thank for this?'

'I really couldn't say, sir,' Jess said. 'We was just talking about it, that's all.'

Ephraim smiled. 'Well,' he said. 'I'll go and fetch them.' He opened the door again, and to Jess he added, 'After you.'

'You'll come back and see me, won't you?' Stephen called after her. 'You can look through my kaleidoscope all you want.'

Jess would have liked that very much, but she did not have time to respond. As she turned around, Ephraim closed the door behind him with a click.

'Remarkable,' he said as they reached the top of the

staircase together. His face was beaming.

'What is?' Jess asked.

'Why, your influence on my son, of course,' Ephraim said. 'I can scarcely believe my own eyes. I've rarely seen him so calm, and he never takes to strangers.' They began to descend the stairs together, walking slowly. 'Stephen has what one might call an unusual temperament. He's often angry and likes everything just so. Any form of change disturbs him greatly. With his studies, he demonstrates sheer brilliance in some, and yet utter slow-wittedness in others. He should have little need of tutors at his age. He shall be sixteen soon, and yet he still fails to grasp some of the most elementary of subjects. Did he tell you that he draws and paints?'

'No, sir, he never.'

'My, how he paints,' Ephraim continued. He stopped partway down the stairs. 'I had that kaleidoscope made especially for him. I did so because from an early age I noticed that he'd taken an interest in patterns – and the more complex the better. He hadn't had it five minutes when he began drawing the patterns he saw through it, and he would colour them in, exactly as he saw them. Perhaps the most remarkable thing is that he only had to see the pattern once. I later tested him to be sure. I set the kaleidoscope on one of my tripods and had him look at the pattern I created. Then I asked him to reproduce it. It took him just two days, off and on, and it was exact in every tiny detail.'

'That's amazing,' Jess said. 'You and your missus must be very proud of him.'

'Indeed I am,' Ephraim said. 'As was his mother, while she was alive.'

'I'm sorry.'

They continued walking. 'There's no need to apologise. Disease took her from us several years ago now – through no one's fault but her own, I might add. She was bent on helping the poor and needy as much as she could, and to her credit, I suppose, no words from me could dissuade her. Her charitable work frequently took her into such unsanitary conditions that it ultimately killed her.'

'I know what you mean.'

'You do?'

Jess nodded. 'I've lost two brothers and a sister the same way. They never made it to their first birthday, the poor lambs, and we got it better than most in our area.'

They reached the bottom of the stairs and Ephraim stopped again. 'And where is that?' he said, looking down at her with his eyebrows raised. 'That is to say, where exactly do you live?'

The question made Jess wary. She did not wish to tell him where she lived, in case he sent for her father to take her back. 'Begging your pardon, sir, but I don't live nowhere no more.'

Ephraim eyed the bundle she still had clenched in her hand. 'I thought that might be the case,' he said. 'You've run away from home, haven't you?'

Jess nodded. 'I ain't going back, neither.'

'And why is that, if you don't mind me asking?'

Jess did not answer straight away. She thought about the reason, going over what would have happened to her if she'd stayed, or ever went back there again. 'There was a man coming for me,' she said a moment later. 'A man was to give my father some money for me. Then I was to marry him, only I heard he never married anyone, and I wasn't the first. I know nothing good will become of me if I go back.'

'My, my,' Ephraim said. 'This is most disturbing. And who is this man?'

'I'd rather not say, sir. I don't want no trouble.'

'But where will you go?'

Jess shrugged her shoulders. 'Not really thought much about that,' she said, 'but anywhere's better than that place.'

Ephraim drew a long and thoughtful breath. A moment later, he pointed across the hallway to the front door and said, 'My late wife, Eudora, would never forgive me if I let you walk out of that door. At least, not until you've made a sensible plan about where you intend to go.' He lowered his arm and smiled at Jess. 'And I would never forgive myself for denying Stephen his new-found friend. Why don't you stay here with us until you've decided what to do?'

Jess suddenly found herself holding her breath. She just stared at Ephraim, too choked to answer. She had never before known such kindness as she had experienced since leaving Pottery Lane, first from Irish Maggie, and now from this man whose house she had entered without invitation.

Taking her silence for hesitation, Ephraim said, 'It's an entirely selfish proposition on my part, I know, for Stephen's sake, but would you like that?'

Jess swallowed the lump that had risen in her throat. Then, with tears welling in her eyes, she nodded and said, 'Yes please, sir. I should like that very much.'

CHAPTER SIXTEEN

Present day

Jefferson Tayte was standing beside Nat outside a rundown terraced house in Brixton, looking up at the dirty windows and peeling paintwork that, according to the Companies House database they had obtained the address from, was the home of Lawrence Black, the second of S E Black's descendants they hoped to talk to. It was a little after one-thirty in the afternoon, not long after Tayte had finished his Saturday morning class and said goodbye to Inspector Dalton. With enough luck, he thought they would have time to visit all three remaining family members that afternoon. To make things easier, they planned to visit each of them in order of their geographical location, from Brixton to Putney, and then Hammersmith.

Although Tayte was fully aware that he was now part of a police investigation as far as Inspector Dalton was concerned, he intended to stick to what he did best and focus on finding out what had become of Jessie Bates. Having been told by Brendan Black that his sister had taken on their father's house after he died, presumably with all it contained at the time, he was all the more keen to visit her home in Hammersmith. Maybe she'd come across something in the attic that might prove useful to his and Nat's research. Right now, though, he was keen to have Lawrence Black answer his front door. He'd tried the doorbell several times without luck. Now he began to rap his knuckles on one of the door's frosted glass panels.

'I know you're home,' he said under his breath.

When he'd knocked the first time, Nat had seen the yellowing net curtains twitch. Someone was definitely there.

'Mr Black!' Tayte called out, the volume of his voice and his American accent drawing attention from the passers-by in the street behind him. 'We'd just like to talk to you about your ancestor, Stephen Black. We won't keep you long.'

Nat edged closer to him. 'I don't think he's going to answer,' she said. 'Perhaps we'd better go.'

Tayte gave a sigh. 'I'm not giving up just yet,' he said. His briefcase was growing heavy on his arm. He put it down at his feet. 'I don't like being so persistent, but it irks me to know he's home and doesn't have the courtesy to answer his door, even if it's just to tell us to go away.'

He rang the doorbell and knocked again, a little louder this time. He figured the occupant would grow tired of hearing him knocking and calling his name sooner or later.

'Do you know you have a hole in your briefcase?' Nat said.

'What's that?' Tayte said, distracted by his mission to get Lawrence Black to answer his door. He followed Nat's eyes down to the side of his briefcase. 'Oh, that,' he added. 'Believe it or not, that's a bullet hole.'

'Really? Someone shot at you?'

Tayte's thoughts drifted back to the occasion. 'I know, right? Who would want to shoot a genealogist?' He made light of it now, but that, and a few other narrow scrapes, was part of the reason he was now teaching. 'It was right here in London,' he added, 'but don't worry, the good guys won.' He sighed as he thought about Marcus Brown. 'Well, maybe not all the good guys.'

He swallowed the lump that had suddenly risen in his throat and knocked on the door again. 'Mr Black!' he called a second time, and now he saw a shadow moving beyond the glass. A moment later, the door cracked open.

'Piss off! I don't want to talk to you.'

'But you don't even know who I am,' Tayte protested.

'Yes, I do. You were on TV last night. I've got nothing to say to you, so bugger off and stop making a commotion on my doorstep!'

Tayte thought it was a reasonable request. He had been rather loud, and had drawn the attention of just about everyone within earshot. Experience told him he wasn't going to get anywhere with Lawrence Black, but at least the man had answered his door. Before the door closed, Tayte quickly reached into his jacket pocket and withdrew Nat's photo of her stolen painting. He pushed it in through the gap, hoping not to get his fingers crushed.

'We're just trying to find out about the girl in this painting,' he said, and again the door eased open a little. 'Just take a look, will you? Your ancestor, Stephen Black, painted it. It's called "Jess". Have you ever heard of her, or the painting?'

To Tayte's surprise, the photograph was suddenly

snatched from his hand. He picked up his briefcase and retreated, thinking that Lawrence Black was taking a good look at it. A second later, however, the door was slammed in his face and the photograph was ejected through the letterbox.

'I don't know anything about it,' Lawrence Black said, his voice muffled on the other side of the door. 'Now clear off before I call the police!'

Tayte picked up the photograph, smoothed it out and put it back inside his jacket. He stepped away and Nat followed after him.

'Maybe I've lost my touch,' he said. 'Perhaps you'd better try the next one.'

They walked back to the pavement.

'I don't think he would have spoken to me, either,' Nat said. 'Do you think he's got something to hide?'

'Who knows?' Tayte said, rummaging in one of the side pockets of his jacket. He took out a couple of Hershey's Miniatures and offered Nat the choice, quietly hoping she would leave his favourite, the yellow-wrapped Mr Goodbar, for him.

'Thanks,' she said, taking the red one.

Tayte popped his chocolate into his mouth, glanced back at the house one last time, and saw movement at the window, letting him know they were still being watched. He looked up at the shabby state of the place again. 'It certainly looks like he could use the money,' he mused, 'but that doesn't necessarily make him a killer or a thief.'

'No, of course not,' Nat said. 'He did seem very touchy, though, and more than a bit upset at us for going to see him.'

Tayte smiled to himself, thinking he'd been met with

far worse in the past. He'd been threatened with shotguns and had dogs set on him before now. 'Come on,' he said as they headed back to the Tube station. 'Let's head over to Putney. Maybe Geoffrey Black will be happier to see us.'

❖ ❖ ❖

Geoffrey Black lived in a small end-of-terrace house in the quiet residential Dover House Conservation Area of Putney, which was to the west of Brixton, where Tayte and Nat had just come from. Unlike the house there, Tayte thought this an attractive, well-maintained home, with a pretty red-tiled roof into which dormer windows were set, and a small front garden with a wooden gate between waist-high hedges. He opened it for Nat, and at the same time he crossed his fingers, hoping again that this visit would be met with a more favourable reception than the last.

'After you,' Tayte said with a smile and a theatrical bow of his head.

'Why thank you, kind sir,' Nat replied, trying not to laugh as she went along with him.

When they reached the front door, Tayte took a step back. 'Your turn,' he said, inviting Nat to ring the doorbell.

Nat froze. 'I thought you were kidding. What shall I say?'

'Just say who you are and why you're here,' Tayte said. 'Like I just did – eventually.'

'You do it,' Nat said, stepping back alongside him.

Tayte gave her a disappointed yet playful look as he leaned forward and pressed the button. Inside the house, Big Ben began to chime. 'Scaredy-cat,' he said. 'I thought this was your assignment. You're definitely doing the next one.'

The door opened before Nat had the opportunity to reply. Standing on the threshold was a trim, grey-haired man in his early fifties, wearing a blue Oxford shirt and beige chinos. He squared his glasses to get a better look at them. A moment later he said, 'Sorry, I'm not interested,' and began to close the door.

Tayte could only imagine he must have thought they were there to sell him something, a middle-aged man with a briefcase and a woman who looked young enough to be his daughter – their religion, perhaps. Before the door closed, he stepped forward and said, 'We're here about one of your ancestor's paintings. I'm a genealogy teacher, and this is one of my students.' He quickly offered a calling card through the gap. 'Are you Geoffrey Black?'

The door opened again. 'I am,' the man said. He began to fiddle with his glasses as before, now studying Tayte more closely. 'Ah yes,' he added. 'I know who you are. I saw you on TV last night.'

'Seems a lot of people did,' Tayte said. 'I was hoping we could come in and talk to you about the painting, and the artist, Stephen Black.'

'It's not a good time,' Black said. 'My wife's not feeling well. She's having a lie-down on the sofa and I don't want to disturb her.'

'I'm sorry to hear that,' Tayte said.

'Migraine,' Black said. 'Look, I'm afraid I know little more about my famous artist ancestor than you can read online, and I know nothing at all about that painting.'

'That's too bad,' Tayte said. 'We're trying to understand the relationship between your ancestor and the girl in the painting, in the hope that we can find out what became of her.'

Nat stepped forward. 'We spoke to your brother, Brendan, yesterday. He was very helpful.'

'Was he?' Black said.

Nat gave a nod. 'He said there was an old trunk of papers left in your late father's attic.'

'Yes, I seem to recall it,' Black said. 'I'm afraid I don't have any of those old papers, though. You'll need to ask our sister about those.'

'That's what your brother told us,' Tayte said. 'We're hoping to see her next.' He took out Nat's photograph of the painting. 'As you saw me talking about the painting on TV last night, you already know it's valuable and that it was recently stolen. Would you mind taking a closer look at it?' He offered it up. 'Have you ever seen this painting before, or heard of it? Perhaps your father mentioned it.'

Black studied the photograph. He shook his head. 'No,' he said. 'The first time I became aware of its existence was when I switched on the news last night.'

'And you know nothing about the girl your ancestor painted?' Tayte asked. 'We're running with the idea that she may have been adopted, perhaps into your family. Ultimately, we're trying to prove it, or as I've said, find out what became of her.'

Black shook his head again. 'No,' he repeated, 'I've never heard any mention of this Jess girl, not from my father or anyone else.' He began to close the door. 'Now, if you'll excuse me, I'm afraid I'm going to have to ask you to leave before we disturb my wife.'

'Well, thanks for your time,' Tayte said as the door closed.

Nat sighed. 'That wasn't very productive, either, was it?'

'At least he had the courtesy to answer his door and speak to us,' Tayte said as they went back out through the gate. 'Talking to the family is an essential part of the process, even if it doesn't always yield results. Besides,' he added, 'it wasn't a complete waste of time.'

'It wasn't?'

'Of course not,' Tayte said. 'We've just spoken to another family member who knows his father had an old trunk full of papers in the attic – at the home we're now going to visit. What are the odds that their sister hasn't gone through it? I mean, who wouldn't?'

'Slim to none,' Nat said, a spring in her step now as they headed along the pavement for the Tube station.

'Exactly,' Tayte said, trying to keep up. 'And if she has, if there is something in there that mentions Jess or the painting, she's sure to have come across it.'

CHAPTER SEVENTEEN

South Kensington, London
1891

It was late. Before Jess ran away from home, she had rarely been up past eight o'clock, unless it was to see to the twins when they woke up crying in the middle of the night. The hours beyond eight o'clock were strictly for the grown-ups, but not any more. It was now past ten, and she was with Ephraim Black in his observatory, as he called it, by special invitation to look into the heavens. The lamps were dimmed, the room in near darkness. Above her, the glass hatch in the cupola was open.

'Almost ready,' Ephraim said, looking into the eyepiece of the smaller finder scope, which sat above the main telescope, as he turned one of the cogged brass wheels. 'You're in for a treat,' he added. 'The air tonight is as clear as I've seen it in weeks.' He held his breath. 'There!' he exclaimed. He stepped away, inviting Jess to take his place. 'Have a look at that and tell me if it isn't the most incredible thing you've ever seen.'

Jess put her eye to the telescope, blinking a few times as her eyelashes brushed the eyepiece. Once she steadied herself, she saw many bright lights in the dark night sky, like fairy dust, or so she imagined. At the centre was a larger, brighter light that seemed to sit within a cloud.

'You're looking at the Crab Nebula,' Ephraim said, his tone full of enthusiasm. 'It's called that because the shape rather resembles the shell of a crab, don't you think?'

'Just like the ones I've seen on the bank of the Thames,' Jess said, trying not to nod her head in case she lost the image. 'Mum took me there on the horse-bus once, when I was little.'

'In a far less evocative fashion,' Ephraim continued, 'we also call it M1 after the French astronomer, Charles Messier. He catalogued a great number of these celestial objects.'

Jess turned to him. 'It's beautiful,' she said. Then she screwed her face up. 'What's a nebula?'

'That's a very good question,' Ephraim said. 'The more we ask, the more we learn. Nebulae are in essence enormous clouds of dust and ionised gases, such as hydrogen and helium. It is believed that within nebulae, new stars are formed. What you're looking at here is the result of a supernova.'

'A supernova?'

'An exploding star!' Ephraim said, throwing his hands out as if to simulate the explosion. 'The supernova was first seen almost nine hundred years ago, and what you see through that telescope today is all the debris from that explosion, still expanding into space. Technically, of course, what you see through that telescope isn't really happening now because the Crab Nebula is several thousand light years away, but we shall keep that subject for another time.'

'Can I please look again?' Jess asked. She didn't understand much of what she was being told, but she was nonetheless fascinated by what she saw.

Ephraim smiled. 'I wish my son exhibited such enthusiasm for my hobby,' he said. 'Yes, by all means. Look for as long as you like. Then I'll find something else for you to see. The Great Globular Cluster in Hercules, perhaps.'

Jess returned her eye to the telescope's eyepiece, and she suddenly felt very small. She wondered how far away the Crab Nebula was, and whether anyone up there was looking back at her. She didn't exactly know why, but it made her think of little Charlie, Hannah and the twins. She hoped with all her heart that they were not suffering because of her, although deep down she knew that poor Charlie would have taken a good thrashing for what she had done.

'You know, you could learn about the stars,' Ephraim said thoughtfully. 'If you wanted to, that is.'

Jess took her eye away from the telescope again. 'Not me,' she said, laughing a little at the suggestion. 'I already told you, I can't even read, and you can't stand around telling me stuff all day.'

'You can't read now,' Ephraim said, 'but you could learn to do that, too.' He waved his hands around him at all the books on the bookshelves. 'Then you would be able to read all of these books, and in time, come to understand them.'

'But I'm just a girl,' Jess said. 'What business do I have with your astronomy?'

'Just a girl!' Ephraim said, sounding affronted, as if he did so on behalf of every woman who ever dared to dream. 'May I remind you, young lady, that the very first book you pulled from these shelves was written by a woman. Furthermore, Agnes Clerke was *just a girl* when she began her lifelong affair with the stars, and she was only a few years older than you are now when she began to write her *Popular History of Astronomy*. What do you say to that?'

Jess didn't say anything, but she did smile at the thought. Could she really learn so much? She began to think she might at least like to try.

Ephraim let out a thoughtful sigh. 'I take it you still have no idea where you intend to go from here?'

'I'm still working on it,' Jess said, and she immediately bit her lip for lying. She didn't like lying to Ephraim Black. He deserved better for his kindness. In truth, she hadn't given the matter a single thought since the day she arrived.

'Well, how's this for a suggestion?' Ephraim said. 'Perhaps you have already reached your destination.'

Jess furrowed her brow as she thought about that. What was he saying?

Ephraim elaborated. 'If you will accept that there is no better place for you to be just now – that is to say, if you will agree to stay here with Stephen and me, then I will commit to your education. In the afternoons, you will learn how to read and write and so forth, and at night, I will teach you all about the cosmos. Would you like that?'

Jess was lost for words. She nodded. She thought she would like that very much indeed, but her throat was suddenly too dry to answer.

'Excellent!' Ephraim said, his face beaming.

'I'd have to work for it, mind,' Jess said, feeling a strong urge to give back what little she could. She was used to hard work. Harder, she supposed, than Ephraim Black could ever demand of her. 'I know I have plenty of learning to do, but when I ain't learning stuff, I'll have to help out – make the beds and peel the spuds, run errands and whatnot.'

'As you wish,' Ephraim said. 'And we must also look into your elocution.'

'My elo-what?'

'Enunciation?'

Jess yawned and just stared at him.

He smiled. 'Never mind. You shall learn the meaning of all these words in time. Now, I see you're getting tired. Perhaps we had better continue our nocturnal studies another time.'

Ephraim went to one of the lamps and turned it up, illuminating the room, and something else that caught Jess's eye.

'Did Stephen paint that?' she asked, pointing to a gilt-framed painting that hung over the unlit fireplace.

Ephraim looked up at the painting with her. 'Yes, he did. It's quite remarkable really. To my knowledge, Stephen has only once looked through my telescope. From that single glance, he painted this.'

'He really don't much care for all this then?'

'Sadly, not,' Ephraim said. 'I'm afraid he far prefers the images he sees in his kaleidoscope.'

Jess squinted at the painting, trying to understand what she was looking at. There were a lot of stars, painted in white, blue and magenta, among other colours. She thought it was just like the image she had seen through the telescope, only the pattern was very different, as if the eye of the telescope had been trained on another part of the cosmos, as she remembered Mr Black had called it.

'What exactly is it a painting of?' she asked.

'This is a painting of what is called a constellation,' Ephraim said. 'In this case, Orion, after the hunter in Greek mythology.' He pointed to a section of the painting towards the middle. 'These three brighter stars form Orion's Belt. Beneath it, coloured magenta here, is the Orion Nebula.'

'Nebula,' Jess repeated, smiling back at him. She liked that word. It was one she knew she would never forget.

'That's right,' Ephraim said, laughing to himself. He went on to indicate more stars on the painting, pointing to each in turn. 'All these brighter stars you see, among those that are less visible, make up the constellation, which is just another word for a group of stars that form a recognisable pattern in the night sky. Even more remarkably, Stephen painted them all with great precision in regard to their relative distance.'

'From just one look?' Jess said, still taking the painting in.

'A few seconds. No more,' Ephraim said. 'And that was all it took for him to realise that my telescope was far less interesting to him than his kaleidoscope.'

'Why did he paint it then? I mean, if he wasn't interested in what he saw.'

Ephraim sighed, as if he wasn't really sure. 'Because he could, I suppose.'

Jess couldn't help but feel a little sorry for Ephraim Black, whom she thought would have loved his son to share his passion for the stars. It seemed, however, that by accepting his offer to remain there with him and Stephen indefinitely, she might in time be able to fill that role, and by doing so give this man, who had been so kind to her, a companion with whom to share his enthusiasm.

They would be good for one another.

Jess started yawning again.

'Dear, dear,' Ephraim said. 'I think I must have kept you up far too late. Off to bed with you. We shall continue your education of the universe another day.'

'Universe?' Jess repeated.

Ephraim laughed as he rested his hand on her shoulder and led her to the door. 'Another day,' he repeated.

CHAPTER EIGHTEEN

Present day

Now north of the Thames, Tayte and Nat emerged from the underground Tube network at Ravenscourt Park in the London Borough of Hammersmith and Fulham, and headed off in the afternoon sunshine in search of the address they were looking for. Five minutes later, thanks to the navigation app on Nat's phone, they were standing outside another terraced house – this one a bay-fronted, red-brick Victorian property at the end of the terrace, with a low-walled garden at the front. There was a shiny silver Jaguar parked alongside the kerb immediately outside – a recently registered, all-electric model, Tayte noticed. That, and the house in this area of West London, told Tayte that Felicity Greenwood at least appeared to be financially better off than any of her siblings, which he supposed was how she had been able to buy her brothers out and keep their late father's house instead of selling it and splitting the proceeds.

Nat opened the gate for Tayte this time. 'Maybe you're right,' she said, grinning. 'Perhaps I'd better do the talking this time. Two out of three visits and we've not been offered so much as a single biscuit between us.'

Tayte laughed. 'Good thing I brought a pocketful of Hershey's then.' They had shared most of them as they walked between one Tube station and another to this house and that. 'Have you gotten a taste for them yet?'

'They're all right,' Nat said. 'Don't you like European chocolate? It must be easier to come by now you live in England.'

'Let's just say that I'm a creature of habit,' Tayte said as they walked the short path to the front door. 'And I have my sources. You'd be surprised how easy they are to get.'

When they arrived at the front door, Tayte held back, inviting Nat to step forward and ring the doorbell. He listened, wondering what tune this one would play. He was disappointed when all he heard was a generic two-tone *Bing-bong!*

'You can do this,' he told Nat when he saw a figure approaching on the other side of the glass.

'I know,' Nat said. 'Be quiet. I have to concentrate.'

Tayte smiled to himself and tried as best he could to shrink into her shadow. Being a heavy-set man over six feet tall, he failed miserably.

When the door opened, a middle-aged woman, with a small, shivering dog in her arms, greeted them. Like her brothers, Tayte put her somewhere in her fifties, although she gave the initial impression that she was trying to look younger. She had short blonde hair and an overly made-up face, and she was smiling broadly through bright, artificially whitened teeth. Tayte thought the smile was promising, but for now he couldn't seem to get past the shivering dog and how its loose hairs were making a mess of the white Chanel jogging suit the woman was wearing.

'Good afternoon,' Nat said, smiling warmly. 'My name's Natalie. I'm a genealogy student, and this is my teacher, Jefferson Tayte. We're trying to break down a brick wall in my family history, and I was hoping you might be able to help us. Are you Felicity Greenwood?'

The woman's smile faltered. At first, Tayte thought they were going to lose her, but her dazzling smile quickly returned. 'Yes, I am,' she said, now studying both of them with curiosity.

'I had a painting of a girl called Jess,' Nat said. 'I believe she's one of my great-great-grandfather's sisters and we're trying to prove it.'

Tayte leaned forward. 'We also believe she may be connected with your family somehow,' he said, unable to stop himself. He reached into his jacket pocket and handed the photograph to Felicity to take a look.

'I heard about this on the news last night,' she said, studying the picture. 'How fascinating. Perhaps you'd better come in. I've just put the kettle on.'

Nicely done, Nat, Tayte thought as Felicity stepped back, inviting them into her home. Just before they entered, he couldn't help but notice the playfully smug look Nat gave him, which was as much as to say that now she'd done the talking they would get their biscuit, and perhaps a whole lot more besides.

Inside Felicity Greenwood's home, the decor was not at all what Tayte expected. It was surprisingly modern, predominantly white with grey accents here and there, colourful Warhol-style pop art on the walls, and lots of glass – from coloured sculpted vases to the clear coffee table they were invited to sit around.

'Sit tight, and I'll bring us a pot of tea,' Felicity said, setting her dog gently down on the light grey carpet. 'Do either of you take sugar?'

Tayte put his hand up. He'd grown to like a good strong cup of English tea over the years. He'd tried to cut out the sugar several times, but found he just didn't enjoy the drink without it. He still preferred coffee, but now they had come this far and had actually been invited into the home of one of Stephen Black's descendants, he didn't want to put anyone out or push his luck.

When Felicity returned to the sitting room, just a couple of minutes later, she set a tray down on the table with the teapot, the milk jug, the cups and sugar bowl, and a side plate full of biscuits. Nat was already smiling at them – at the trophy they had come to represent. Tayte tried not to.

'Do you want to help yourselves, or shall I pour?' Felicity asked, although she had already begun to do just that. 'This is so exciting!' she said. 'To think, Mr Tayte, that you were on television just last night, and now here you are in my sitting room.' She paused, hovering the spout of the white china teapot over Tayte's cup. 'But however did you discover where I live?' she added as she continued to pour. 'Did you use your genealogical skills to find me?'

'Actually, it was far more straightforward than that,' Tayte said, aware of the dog sniffing interestedly at his shoes. 'We obtained your details from the Companies House website, via the fine art prints business your father left to you and your brothers.'

Felicity sat back with her tea, opposite Tayte and Nat, and scoffed. 'That old waste of good retail space,' she said. 'Only my brother Brendan seems to think there's any merit in keeping it going these days. I must get myself taken off the books. I really don't know what he sees in the place. Nostalgia, perhaps.'

'He did seem quite at home there,' Tayte said. 'We saw him yesterday.'

Nat sat forward and helped herself to a biscuit. 'And we've just been to see your other brothers, Lawrence and Geoffrey. Lawrence didn't want to talk to us, and our visit with Geoffrey was very brief.'

Tayte resisted the biscuits and took a mouthful of tea instead. 'There was mention of an old trunk full of papers that your late father left in the attic of this house when he passed,' he said, getting to the point. 'I take it you know of it?'

'Yes, of course,' Felicity said. 'It's huge. I really don't know how he managed to get it up there.'

'It's still there?' Tayte asked, his hopes rising with his tone.

Felicity nodded, distracted momentarily by her dog as it jumped up on to her seat, and then curled up in her lap. 'I couldn't get it down if I tried.'

'That's great,' Tayte said, beaming like a child.

'Have you ever gone through it?' Nat asked.

'Yes, I have,' Felicity said. 'Among other things, there are lots of old astronomy journals as I recall. Stephen's father, Ephraim, was quite accomplished in the field.' She began to fidget excitedly. 'You may also be pleased to know that the name Jess or Jessie rings a bell. I've been thinking about it ever since you mentioned it. I'm sure I've come across the name before, perhaps in connection with the contents of that trunk.'

Felicity was smiling so hard by the time she finished speaking, her voice rising in pitch, that she almost gave a little squeal of excitement at the end. Tayte was right there with her, her words sweet music to his ears.

'I'll have to go through it again,' Felicity continued. 'I can't easily get to it, though, I'm afraid, but if you leave me your number I'll call you as soon as I can. If I find anything, that is.'

'That would be great,' Tayte said. He handed her his card.

'Professional genealogist,' Felicity read out. 'I thought you were a teacher.'

'I am now,' Tayte said, 'but only for the past year. I need to get some new cards made up.' He knew the real reason he was holding on to them was in case teaching didn't work out for him, or he missed the fieldwork too much and decided to go back to it.

Felicity put the card down on the coffee table. 'I'll go up and take a look for you in the morning,' she said. 'I'm having a few friends over for dinner this evening, so I'm afraid I won't be able to get to it any sooner.' She looked at her watch. 'Heavens, is that the time? If there's nothing else you'd like to ask for now, I really must be getting along.'

Tayte drank his tea and put his cup on the tray. He looked at Nat as if to ask whether she could think of anything else to ask. She shook her head, so they both stood up. Tayte knew there would be more questions, but he first had to know what was in that trunk, and how relevant it was to their research.

'I think that will do us for now,' he said. 'Thank you for your time and the tea. Not everyone is so accommodating.'

'My pleasure,' Felicity said. 'It's been pretty quiet around here since my husband died. I've enjoyed your company.'

Tayte offered her a smile. 'Well, we look forward to

hearing from you,' he said, hoping that Felicity would call him soon with news of a discovery – something that might confirm the connection between artist and subject that they were looking for.

CHAPTER NINETEEN

South Kensington, London
1891

It was early evening, two weeks after Ephraim Black had invited Jess to stay indefinitely at the house she had previously chanced upon, which, day by day, she was coming to consider her new home. She had finished her self-assigned duties for the day, having run errands to the High Street and back for Mrs Bramley, the housekeeper, and then having helped Mrs Eady in the kitchen, preparing the evening meal and scrubbing the pots and pans. Dinner was a good hour away, so she had gone looking for Stephen for company, as she often did. She found him in one of the attic rooms, where he'd told her he liked to paint because of the light from the skylights. The door was open. She walked in without knocking and saw him sitting at his easel in a pool of light, the evening twilight rendering the room in a soft golden hue.

'What are you painting?' Jess asked, without introduction.

Stephen had his back to her, obscuring his work from view. At the sound of her voice he jumped in his seat a little and pulled a cloth down over his canvas so Jess couldn't see it.

She sidled up beside him. 'What is it?' she said. 'Another one of your kaleidoscope images? Can't I have a look?'

She reached in to lift the cloth and Stephen slapped the back of her hand. 'It's not ready,' he said, not once looking at her as he spoke.

Jess had initially thought he was just shy of her, but she soon learned that he hardly ever looked at anyone, not directly, unless he was angry with him or her about something.

'Suit yourself,' she said. 'I can go again if you don't want me here.'

'No, don't go,' Stephen said. 'I can show you some more of my other paintings, if you like. They're not all from my kaleidoscope. I like painting buildings, too – architecture.'

Jess was not particularly interested in seeing paintings of buildings, however intricate and precise she knew they would be. More and more, she wanted to know what was beneath that cloth on his easel. 'That's all right,' she said. 'I'll be on my way. I'm sure Dot could do with some help setting out the dinner things. A maid's work is never done, so she tells me.' She stepped away and Stephen made a noise in his throat, as if he was about to say something to stop her from going, but couldn't quite say it. She turned around again. 'What was that?' She knew she was teasing him. 'Were you going to say something?'

She saw Stephen swallow hard, as though he had a mouthful of dry food stuck in his throat. If he did have something else to say, then she thought he really was having a difficult time saying it. He was staring at the blank cloth that covered his canvas.

'Was it something about the painting?'

Stephen nodded, and Jess moved closer.

'Well, what is it? If you won't show me, do you want to tell me about it instead? Is that it?'

Stephen swallowed again, and this time as he did so, he turned away. 'It's of you,' he said, slowly turning back to her, still avoiding eye contact, his face suddenly flushed.

'Me?' Jess repeated, laughing to herself. She could feel her own cheeks flushing now. 'Why in heaven would you want to paint me?'

Stephen did not answer right away. When he did, he avoided the question. 'You don't mind, do you? I can stop if you do.'

Jess laughed again. 'I don't mind,' she said. 'Just seems like a waste of good paint and canvas to me. Don't you want me to sit for it, all proper like? I don't mind.'

'I don't need you to sit for it.'

'No, of course you don't. When can I see it?'

'When it's finished.'

Impatient to have a look, Jess was about to ask when that would be, but before she was able to, she heard something that stopped her. Someone was shouting. It was a man's voice. He sounded close by, as if he were standing right outside on the footpath. Jess listened more attentively. A moment later she gasped.

'I know you've got her in there!' the man yelled.

It was her father.

Jess stood and listened to his yelling for several seconds before she was able to move again. Hearing his voice instantly brought back dark memories that she had begun to forget. It froze her to the spot. It had reminded her of where she really belonged, and it immediately shattered her dreams. How had he found her?

'Jess!'

She heard another voice then, echoing in the hallway below. It was Ephraim Black.

Jess looked at Stephen, and although he could not know who was out there, could not understand what it meant, he seemed to sense the fear that had reached in and caught Jess in its cold grasp.

'What is it, Jess?' he asked.

'It's my dad,' Jess said. 'He's come to take me back.'

'Jess!'

She heard Ephraim call for her again and she went to the door. She turned back. 'Keep painting me, won't you? That way at least you'll remember me.'

Jess ran out of the room, not stopping until she was at the top of the main staircase that led down into the hall. She saw Ephraim, and then she saw her father in his muddy old boots and his usual tatty attire of old brown trousers and filthy off-white shirt, his sleeves rolled up past his elbows as if ready for a fight. Jess knew she could give him none, and she doubted Ephraim could stand up to him.

Her father had seen her too. 'Get yourself down here right now!' he yelled.

Jess went to him, slowly at first, until he yelled at her again.

'Be quick about it!' he said. 'Ain't you wasted enough of my time already?'

As soon as Jess's foot left the last step, Harry Bates lunged at her. He grabbed her upper arm, squeezing it until she thought it might break. Then he yanked her along with him towards the open front door. She caught

Ephraim's eye as he stepped forward to intervene, his face aghast.

'Now, there's no need—' Ephraim began, but Harry cut him short.

'No need for what?' he said, shoving Jess behind him as if she weighed no more than a rag doll. He stepped closer to Ephraim, until he was within arm's reach. His jaw jutted out. His teeth were clenched. 'You would do well to mind your business and leave me to mine,' he warned.

Jess saw him reach into his pocket then, and she knew what he was going for even before he took it out. It was his gamekeeper's priest. He drew it out and held it up in front of Ephraim. He began to waggle the weighted end threateningly in front of him.

'If you don't, you'll get some of what's coming to this little brat!'

Jess saw that, even now, Ephraim was about to say or do something in her defence, but she warned him not to. Behind her father's back she began to shake her head, so frantically, so afraid of what her father might do to Ephraim, that Ephraim could not fail to understand her meaning. She saw him relax again, and so, too, did her father.

'That's right,' Harry said. 'We don't want no trouble now, do we?'

Ephraim looked at Jess, and then back at Harry. He shook his head.

'Good.'

Harry turned around and reasserted his grip on Jess's arm. Then he led her outside at an uncomfortable march. As they paced along the path towards the gate, Jess tried to look back at Ephraim. She was sure he would be watching from the doorstep, but every time she tried to look, her father jerked her around again, denying her a last goodbye.

CHAPTER TWENTY

Present day

'Do you want to get a coffee and go over our progress before we call it a day?' Tayte asked Nat as they headed back to the Tube station, following their visit with Felicity Greenwood. He threw her a grin. 'I think I owe you one after your outstanding doorstep performance back there.'

Nat gave him a dry look. 'As soon as Felicity Greenwood recognised you from your TV appearance last night, she became so excited to see us, I don't think it mattered what I said.'

'True,' Tayte said. 'But you did great. Where do you prefer – Starbucks, Costa or Caffè Nero?'

'I prefer independent coffee shops, but I don't mind.'

'Great. I don't mind, either, so let's call into the first one we come to.'

They found a small family-run Italian restaurant, not far from the Tube station, which had not long opened for the evening. As there was still plenty of warm late-afternoon sunshine to be had, they sat outside on aluminium chairs at a matching table, overlooking the park from which the Ravenscourt Park Tube station took its name. Tayte ordered a double espresso, while Nat went for a latte, sprinkled with hundreds and thousands, which didn't surprise Tayte, given her penchant for colour.

'So what do we have, and where do we go next?' Tayte asked, interested in hearing Nat's take on things so far.

Nat drew a deep breath, as if gathering her thoughts. 'Well, from the Companies House website, and from Brendan Black, we learned that the family business is in trouble, and that he's the only one who still seems to care about it. We also heard about a trunk full of old papers. Lawrence Black wouldn't talk to us, but Geoffrey would – although I think all we got from him was confirmation of the trunk at their late father's house, which Felicity Greenwood now owns. Felicity confirmed she still has it, and is the only one who seems to have heard of Jess, but at the moment that's somewhat tenuous. As to where we go next, I suppose we just have to wait and hope she finds something interesting in that trunk tomorrow.'

'Yup, that about sums it up so far,' Tayte said, sipping his coffee. He wiped the foam from his top lip with the back of his hand. 'But we still have other avenues to follow. We've spoken with the family – the descendants of the artist who painted the portrait of the girl we're interested in. Next we need to look at the records.'

'Which records?' Nat said. 'I think I've dug up just about everything that's out there about Jess. You went over my work yourself.'

'Yes, I did, and as I said, it's great work, but it focuses on your family tree. You've been looking for Jessie Bates and can't find anything about her after the 1891 census. I think we now need to look more closely at the Black family. Maybe we can make a connection that way. First, though, you're right – let's wait until tomorrow to see what, if anything, the contents of that trunk can offer us.'

Tayte drained his coffee back. 'You want another one?'

'I'm fine,' Nat said. 'But you go ahead.'

Tayte ordered another double espresso. By the time it arrived, Nat had her phone out. He imagined she was probably texting her friends, as he found young people always seemed to do these days, but a moment later she started smirking and turned the screen around to show him what she was looking at. It was the local TV news report from the night before, streaming on catch-up TV.

'I missed it last night,' she said. 'With all the people we've visited this afternoon mentioning it, I've been dying to see it.'

'I've been dreading seeing it,' Tayte said, at the same time leaning in for a closer look. 'Am I really that big?'

Nat laughed. 'Don't worry about it. Everyone knows television puts pounds on you.'

Like watching a disaster unfold before one's eyes, Tayte wanted to look away, but he couldn't help himself. The news report hadn't been playing long. He was just walking up the steps outside the Marcus Brown School of Family History.

'Are you Jefferson Tayte?' he heard the reporter ask as she came up behind him. 'Do you mind if I ask you a few questions about the painting you discovered?'

Tayte found himself leaning in even closer. 'Turn it up, would you?'

As he watched and listened, he realised he hadn't really given the reporter much. Most of what she'd said, she already knew from her source, which Tayte knew had to have come from their conversation with the art expert, Barrett Huckabee. Talking with Nat just now about the visits they had made that afternoon to see Stephen Black's descendants had brought their brief conversations back to him. Tayte was very good at remembering what people told him when he went to see them. Now he was thinking about Geoffrey Black and what he'd said. Towards the end of their conversation, he'd said that he'd never heard any mention of Jess, not from his father or anyone else. Tayte hadn't thought anything of it at the time. He'd just assumed that Geoffrey had heard the name, Jess, on the TV news report the night before, along with everyone else, but now, as he listened more closely to the report playing back in front of him, he knew he hadn't once mentioned her name. As the news report ended, it was confirmed.

'I never said her name,' Tayte uttered quietly to himself, but Nat heard him.

'What's that?' she said. 'Whose name?'

'Jess's name. I never once said what the painting was called, or who the subject of the portrait was.'

'Okay, so?'

'So, how come Geoffrey Black knew it?'

Nat pulled a face. 'I'm afraid you've lost me.'

'When we went to see him earlier, just before we left he spoke her name. How could he know it if, as he said, he never knew anything about the painting or the subject?'

'Are you sure?' Nat asked, furrowing her brow. 'Maybe you mentioned it earlier in the conversation.'

Tayte shook his head, going back over in his mind what was said. 'I'm sure I didn't.'

'How sure?'

'Very sure,' Tayte said. 'It was a brief doorstep conversation. I know what I said.' He took out his phone. 'It would appear that Geoffrey Black knows more than he's letting on,' he added. 'I'm calling Inspector Dalton. I think this is the kind of thing he'd like to know about.'

CHAPTER TWENTY-ONE

North Kensington, London
1891

It was dark outside by the time Harry Bates brought Jess home, shivering slightly from the unseasonably cool evening air. Little Charlie ran to her and threw his arms around her as soon as her father shoved her in through the front-room door. She ruffled the lad's bright blonde hair, holding him close, still choking back the tears she had cried all the way back to Pottery Lane. To Jess, the house felt colder than ever now, and it was not because the fire hadn't been lit. Her mother was sitting with the twins in her arms, Hannah standing at her side. Gert's expression was as livid as her father's.

'Look at you, all scrubbed up in that pretty new dress,' she yelled, getting to her feet. 'Where the bloody hell have you been? Don't you know the trouble you've caused? What were you thinking?'

Jess knew she was expected to say she was sorry – that she would behave herself and be a good girl from now on, but she didn't. The only thing she was sorry about was being back there in that heart-rending place.

The twins began to cry, and Gert instinctively bounced them in her arms. 'Selfish! That's what you are, my girl!' she continued. She turned to Harry. 'Have you beaten her yet?'

Harry shoved Jess further into the room and closed the door behind him. 'No,' he said, sounding weary from all the walking he'd been forced to endure on Jess's account, although she knew now that there was nothing at all wrong with his legs. He'd frog-marched her most of the way without a single limp or complaint.

'Well, what are you waiting for?' Gert said. She handed the twins awkwardly to Hannah. 'Take your brother upstairs and go to bed.'

Charlie protested. 'I don't want to go to bed. I want to stay with Jess.'

Harry whipped his gamekeeper's priest out and held it up to Charlie's face. 'You'll get up those stairs sharpish if you know what's good for you, boy!'

'Go on, Charlie,' Jess said. 'And you, Hannah. I'll see you both in the morning.'

At hearing that, her mother gave a contradictory scoff.

As soon as she was left alone with her parents, Jess asked, 'I will be here in the morning, won't I?'

Jess's mother had a baleful look on her face, made all the more sinister by the shadows cast by the lamplight. 'Give her what's coming to her, Harry love. It's for her own good, and well deserved.'

'You know I can't do that,' Harry said.

'Why not?' Jess asked, as if she would rather take the beating than the alternative.

Harry put his gamekeeper's priest away again. 'Because I don't want to spoil those pretty looks of yours, or that nice new dress, that's why. Mr Butterfill is on his way here this very evening with my money to take you off our hands.'

'And good riddance!' Gert chipped in. 'You little horrors are more trouble than you're worth, the lot of you. You wouldn't believe the bother your father's had trying to keep Mr Butterfill interested in you, and a roof over our heads, besides.'

'That's enough, Mother,' Harry said.

Gert sat down again, sighing heavily. 'Lost my job at the match works because of you,' she told Jess, her voice quieter now, seething. 'Had to stay home so your dad could go out looking for you with his cronies.'

'I said, that's enough!' Harry told her. He turned to Jess. 'Sit yourself down on the floor in the corner there and keep quiet. I don't want to give Mr Butterfill spoiled goods if I can help it, but I will if I have to, you hear me?'

Jess did as she was told. She sank into the corner of the room and hugged her knees up close to her chest. In her mind she berated herself over and over for not being more careful. Of course her father had been out looking for her – his friends, too. She knew now one of them must have seen her running her errands to Kensington High Street, and had followed her back to Ephraim Black's house. She should have kept going, she told herself. She should have found another place to stay, far away from Kensington. But what use was hindsight to her now? Mr Butterfill was coming for her, just as before. Nothing had changed.

Half an hour must have passed before there came a knock at the front door.

Harry rubbed his hands together and smiled. 'Here's Mr Butterfill now.'

Jess noted the spring in her father's step as he went to answer the door, but he was wrong. Jess would have heard the tell-tale tap of Mr Butterfill's cane on the pavement long before the knock at the door, and the knock they had just heard was more of a thump than the sharp tap, tap, tap that always preceded his visits. Jess could not see the front door from her corner of the room, but she could listen, and what she heard confirmed her thoughts.

'Harry!' a gruff voice said. 'Well, well. Good of you to open the door to us this time.'

'Does that mean you've got our money?' another, equally gruff voice said. 'I hope for your sake it does.'

There was a pause before Harry answered the two men. He had clearly been caught by surprise. Jess knew why that was. The voices belonged to Frank and John Fuller.

Harry laughed nervously. 'To own the truth, gentlemen,' he said, 'I was expecting someone else.'

'Were you now?' Frank said. 'Did you hear that, John? He wasn't expecting us.'

Harry laughed again. 'That is not to say that I would not have opened the door had I known it was you. I must have been out when you called before.'

Without invitation, the front-room doorway was suddenly filled, first with Frank Fuller's hulking figure, and then with John's. Both men appeared all the larger for the dark greatcoats they were wearing to ward off the evening's chill. Gert immediately shrank into her chair.

'Yes, come in, come in,' Harry said unnecessarily as he followed after them.

'Don't lie to us, Harry,' Frank said. 'You've been avoiding us, plain and simple, and we don't take kindly to it.

We had an agreement, and you've broken it.'

'Yeah,' John said. 'You've been stringing us along for weeks now.'

'Not at all, fellas,' Harry said. 'As I told you before, I've had a few complications, but it's all under control now.' He looked down at Jess. 'See? I've got my eldest back again.'

Neither of the Fuller brothers looked at Jess. They were not interested in her.

'Where's our money?' Frank said, getting to the point.

'It's coming,' Harry said.

John grabbed Harry by the back of his neck and forced their faces together. 'You keep saying that. I'm tired of hearing it.'

'You're a little early, that's all,' Harry said, laughing nervously again.

'Early?' Frank said. He scoffed. 'You'll make me laugh in a minute.'

'You think this is funny?' John said, grimacing at Harry.

'No, John, of course not,' Harry said, his features darkening. 'Mr Butterfill's on his way here now. I swear it. He's coming for Jess, as I told you before. As soon as I've conducted my business with him, we can conclude ours.'

'We'll wait then,' Frank said.

Harry laughed again, and now John slapped him across the face. 'Do that again and I'll conclude our business right here and now, money or not.'

Harry's face instantly reddened in the lamplight. 'My apologies to you both,' he said, suddenly sour-faced. 'It's just that I can't have you here when Mr Butterfill calls. He's a private sort, you know. It would surely jeopardise our arrangement. Can't you come back for your money tomorrow? I'll have it for you first thing in the morning.'

Jess heard John suck the air in through his teeth. Her father was testing his patience further than she thought he ought to.

'There he goes with his excuses again, Frank. He's never going to pay us. He's playing us for fools.'

'Is that right, Harry?' Frank said. 'Do you think we're stupid?'

Harry laughed again. He seemed so nervous now that Jess doubted he could help himself. What happened next came so fast it startled her. She gasped as John pulled a knife from his coat pocket. Then, without so much as taking a breath to consider his actions, he thrust it hard into her father's side. He'd had enough. That much was clear. His eyes widened as he pressed the knife deeper. Harry groaned and sighed. Then he slumped to the floor, slowly, in John Fuller's arms. Gert just watched. She did not scream, nor did she rush to Harry's side as a wife might under the circumstances. She just sat in her chair, quietly taking it all in, although Jess could see that she was shaking with fear.

'John!' Frank said. 'Now, why would you go and do that? For heaven's sake, what's wrong with you?'

'He was a lost cause, Frank, and I don't like being laughed at,' John said, still stooping over Harry as he drew his last breaths. He wiped his knife on Harry's shirt. 'And I was tired of his excuses.'

Frank sighed. He shook his head. Then Jess heard a familiar tapping sound on the pavement outside. She looked at the window and Frank Fuller's eyes followed hers as the sound drew closer. Then came the unmistakeable sound of Mr Butterfill's cane rapping at the front door.

Tap! Tap! Tap!

CHAPTER TWENTY-TWO

Present day

Inspector Dalton had been busy with another case when Tayte called him the day before with his suspicions about Geoffrey Black, but the inspector had been keen to talk to him, not only about Tayte and Nat's findings, but about his own. They had agreed to meet him the following morning at Holborn police station. Upon their arrival, they were taken to an interview room, where Dalton was waiting for them. The inside of a police interview room was nothing new to Tayte, but he could tell that it was Nat's first time. As they entered, she couldn't stop looking around at the pale-blue soundproofed walls and ceiling. There was nothing much else to see, but it seemed to fascinate her.

They sat at a desk, opposite Dalton. As the room was only being used out of convenience, the door remained open, the recording device switched off. Dalton wasn't wearing a suit today, perhaps because it was Sunday. He looked as if he'd been to the gym or out jogging – maybe both. As Tayte settled his briefcase between his feet, he imagined the inspector was fitting in their chat before his shift began, or that he'd had to come in for some other reason, making it convenient for him to meet them there.

'What you told me on the phone yesterday afternoon about Geoffrey Black,' Dalton said, flexing his interlaced hands on the desk in front of them, as if he were still stretching after his workout. 'It's all well and good, but it's not enough to go after him. If it's true, it's highly suspicious, though. I'll give you that.'

Tayte sat forward. 'What do you mean, *if* it's true?' he said, sounding put out. 'It *is* true.'

'What I mean, Mr Tayte, is that he only has to say you mentioned Jess's name when you first arrived, and you can't prove otherwise, can you?' He turned to Nat. 'You were there, Miss Cooper. Was the name of the painting or the subject mentioned prior to Geoffrey Black using it?'

Nat looked at Tayte. 'I couldn't say for sure,' Nat said. 'Sorry,' she added, almost as an apology to Tayte for not being able to back him up.

'And that's the problem,' Dalton said. 'I'm not suggesting you're wrong, but memory can be a funny thing. It's unreliable. All we have here is your word against his that he was caught out by the oldest catch in the book.'

Tayte sat back with a sigh. 'I know what was said and what wasn't said. Geoffrey Black knows something.'

'Maybe he does,' Dalton said. 'But if he is the man we're looking for and I bring him in for questioning based on what you've told me, I know from experience that he'll say you mentioned Jess's name first and I won't get a thing from him. The only thing it will accomplish is to let him know we're on to him. Presumably, whoever has the painting needs to sell it. That won't be easy. Since hearing that Miss Cooper's cousin died from her injuries, turning this art theft into a murder investigation, I'm sure whoever's behind it is keeping their head down for now, waiting for things to cool off. If I go poking around without enough evidence to charge someone, that painting may never surface again.' Dalton took a deep breath and relaxed back into his chair. 'But don't worry. We're watching them.'

'You think you'll catch whoever it is when he comes to sell the painting?' Nat said.

'Perhaps,' Dalton said. 'It's worth a lot of money. The sale of such an item is bound to make some noise, and as I see it, almost all of the Black family could use the money – not that already having money precludes a person from wanting more.'

'Almost all?' Tayte said, seeking clarification.

'Brendan Black. He's not too hard up. His motive seems to lie more with setting things right, as he might see it.'

'We heard he put up quite a fight over the S E Black painting their father had,' Tayte said, 'when the family contested their late father's will.'

Dalton chuckled to himself. 'Fight is the word,' he said. 'Did you know that by the end of the day, he'd assaulted three people – one of them a female police officer who was trying to calm him down?'

Tayte and Nat both shook their heads in disbelief.

'How about Felicity Greenwood?' Tayte said. 'She seemed very well off to me.'

'All an illusion,' Dalton said. 'Her husband died, leaving her in a lot of debt. On top of that she has several credit cards, all at their limit. She appears to enjoy the good things in life, but she's living well beyond her means. However, before your cousin died, Miss Cooper, she was able to tell us it was a man who broke into her house that day.'

'Lawrence Black seemed to need the money most,' Nat said. 'He wouldn't talk to us, either. I know that doesn't necessarily mean anything.'

'Ah, Lawrence Black. Charges of possession and assault ten years ago. A string of low-paid jobs he never seems to stick at. We've been doing our homework. Yes, money could be a great motivator for him, but coming back to Geoffrey Black, he could use the money, too.'

'I thought he seemed nicely set up,' Tayte said.

'He was made redundant several months ago. He was in Information Technology. I'm sure it must be getting tough for him by now. There's plenty of much younger competition out there.'

'What about his wife? Doesn't she go out to work?'

'He's not married.'

Tayte felt a tingle on the back of his neck. He and Nat exchanged glances. 'He told us his wife was feeling unwell.'

'A migraine,' Nat added.

'Did he now?' Dalton said, his considerable muscles flexing beneath his sweatshirt. He rubbed thoughtfully at his stubble. 'Geoffrey Black grows more and more suspicious, doesn't he?'

'Yes, he does,' Tayte agreed, thinking that if Dalton wasn't going to bring him in just yet, to ask him why he'd lied to them about his wife and have him explain how he knew the name Jess, then he wanted to go back to see him and ask a few more questions of his own. He was just wondering how he could put a genealogical spin on those questions when his phone rang, playing a show tune from *Oklahoma*.

He took it out from his suit-jacket pocket. 'Excuse me,' he said as he read the display. He didn't recognise the number. The caller wasn't on his contacts list, but the number told him it was from somewhere in London. 'I need to take this,' he added, looking at Nat. 'I think it could be Felicity Greenwood. I believe she may have some information for us.'

CHAPTER TWENTY-THREE

North Kensington, London
1891

At the house on Pottery Lane, all eyes turned towards the front door as Mr Butterfill's cane continued to rap against the wood. Jess wondered what the Fuller brothers would do. With her father's dead body lying at their feet, surely they would pretend there was no one home, in the hope that the caller would go on his way again. But the lamp was lit. Mr Butterfill would have seen its light glowing at the window.

Tap! Tap! Tap! 'Damn it, Bates!' Butterfill called. 'Must I stand out here all night?'

'Let him in,' Frank told Gert.

'Are you sure, Frank?' John said, looking down at Harry's lifeless body.

Frank did not answer. He looked at Gert again. 'I said, let him in. If you try to warn him, I'll kill you both.'

Gert stood up, still shaking from the shock of seeing John Fuller murder her husband. Jess watched her leave the room to answer the door, moving at a snail's pace. She thought her mother seemed to have aged ten years in a single evening.

Tap! Tap! Tap!

'I'm coming!' Gert called, although her words were little more than a whisper.

Frank followed her out while John stood against the wall, to one side of the front-room door.

Jess heard her mother lift the catch, then Mr Butterfill's protestations.

'What in heaven kept you so long, woman?' he said, his voice raised. 'I would have thought you and your husband would be keen to welcome me in on this evening of all evenings.'

Gert did not answer. She had no time to. The next thing Jess heard was the front door as it slammed shut. It was quickly followed by Frank Fuller's voice.

'Get in there!' he yelled, and Mr Butterfill was suddenly thrust into the room, bent almost double, his glasses askew on his face. John grabbed him. He pulled his knife out again and pinned the now very disturbed-looking Mr Butterfill against the wall. He pressed his knife to Butterfill's throat.

'And who might you be?' John asked him.

'B-Butterfill,' came a stammering answer.

'Well, well,' John said. To his brother he added, 'Seems Harry was telling us the truth this time.'

'I figured it had to be him,' Frank said, studying Butterfill's pointed features. 'Looks like we're going to get paid after all.'

John sneered. 'Got some money for us, have you?'

Butterfill tried to shake his head, but John pressed his knife harder against his skin. It made Butterfill think again about lying to these people. He nodded instead.

'Inside my coat pocket,' Butterfill said. 'Take it all and

I'll be on my way.'

From her corner of the room, Jess had a clear view of everything that was going on. She could see that Mr Butterfill kept staring down at her father's dead body. He'd seen too much, as she and her mother surely had.

'I don't think so,' Frank said, foraging inside Butterfill's coat for the money he'd brought to pay Harry for his daughter. He pulled out a bundle of banknotes, stood back and rifled through it. Then he gave John a subtle nod.

'I know what you are,' John said to Butterfill.

Butterfill began to shake his head, his eyes wide with fear.

John tilted his head towards Jess. 'I know what you do to the likes of this poor young girl sitting in the corner there. Believe me when I say that this gives me great pleasure.'

With that, John Fuller drew the blade of his knife across Mr Butterfill's throat and held him up against the wall, staring into his fading eyes until the life was gone from them.

Jess gasped and put her hand to her mouth. Across the room, silently taking it all in as she was, her mother did the same. Neither dared to scream – did not dare to draw attention to themselves. Were they to be next? Jess tried not to think about it. She pulled her knees up tighter to her chest.

Frank Fuller turned to them. 'I've never killed a child,' he said, 'and neither has John here, have you, John?'

'No, Frank,' John said, cleaning the blood off his knife for the second time that evening.

'Come to think of it,' Frank continued, 'I've only ever killed one woman in all the forty-something years of my life.' He looked hard at Jess, and then he fixed the same dark stare on her mother. 'I'd like to keep it that way. Do you think that's possible?'

Jess and her mother began to nod firmly.

'Good,' Frank said. 'Now, if you do as I tell you, there'll be no need to burden my conscience further, will there?'

Neither Jess nor her mother answered.

'I said, will there?' Frank repeated.

'No,' Jess and her mother said together, their voices little more than whimpers.

'So here's what happened,' Frank said. 'We was never here. The landlord, Butterfill, called on you for his rent money, but Harry couldn't pay him. You was all going to be out on your ear, but Harry was having none of it. They got into a row and then a fight. Butterfill pulled a knife – a rent collector's got to have some protection, especially around here. He stabbed Harry, but it didn't kill him, not at first. Harry then wrestled the knife off Butterfill and cut his throat with it, right before he died himself.' He turned to John, who was just putting his knife away. 'You'll have to leave the knife, John.'

'But it's my favourite.'

'Well, I'm not carrying one. Have you got a spare tucked away somewhere?'

John shook his head, frowning.

'So drop the bloody knife.'

John stooped down and smeared some of Butterfill's blood on to the blade he'd just cleaned. He dropped it on the floor between the two men.

'That's it then,' Frank said. He turned to Jess and her mother again, a dry smile on his face. 'The scene is set, and you both know what to tell the peelers.' He flicked through the wad of banknotes he'd taken from Mr Butterfill. He handed some of the money to Gert. 'That's for your trouble. Better than a simple handshake on our agreement, wouldn't you say?'

Jess watched her mother's eyes light up at the sight of what must have amounted to several months' wages from the match works. Gert rolled it up and held it tightly in her fist. 'You have my word that neither you nor your brother was ever here,' she said. 'Ain't that right, Jess?'

Frank's eyes were on Jess that instant. She nodded. She did not wish to share her father's fate, or that of Mr Butterfill. She owed them nothing. As far as Jess was concerned, both men had received their just deserts.

Frank turned away. 'Come on, John. Let's get out of here.'

Jess watched them leave, but even before they had closed the front door behind them, her mother began to distract her. She was counting the money she'd been given, all the while smiling to herself. Then she proceeded to gather up a few things in her arms: the small clock from the mantel that had been her mother's, her shawl from the back of her chair.

'What are you doing?' Jess asked her, puzzled.

'I'm leaving,' Gert said, too busy deciding what to grab next to give Jess so much as a glance.

'Leaving?'

'That's right, and why shouldn't I? I've had to put up with your father all these years, haven't I? Well, now he's gone and I can't take it no more. As for you kids – I'm washing my hands of the lot of you.'

Jess couldn't believe what she was hearing. Was her mother really going to abandon them? 'What about Hannah and Charlie?' she said. 'What about the twins?'

Gert laughed the laugh of a mad woman who could no longer accept the realities of her life. 'I can hardly take them with me, can I? You'll have to take care of them. You've managed so far.'

Jess shook her head. A part of her wanted to slip out after her mother and go back to Ephraim Black. She had a fine home waiting for her if she wanted it. All she had to do was go – leave all this behind and never look back. But how could she? This wasn't like before. When she ran away before, her parents, for what good they were, had been there to take some sort of care of her siblings. Now, with her father dead and her mother running off to goodness knows where, Jess was all her siblings had.

'We'll be sent to the workhouse,' Jess said. She knew she could not let Hannah and Charlie share that fate without her, while she was eating three good meals a day under Ephraim Black's roof. 'Heaven knows what'll happen to the twins.'

'That ain't my problem no more,' Gert said, putting down a jug she'd previously picked up, presumably having decided it was one item too many. She could only carry so much.

She went to the door, not once looking Jess in the eyes. She paused briefly. Then she left without another word, or a kiss goodbye for any of her children.

CHAPTER TWENTY-FOUR

Jess had no idea how long had passed when the sound of voices on the street outside disturbed her from her thoughts. Since her mother had run off, abandoning her and her siblings to their fates, she had continued to sit in the corner of the front room, shivering, with her arms wrapped tightly around her knees, wondering what to do. She wanted to move. She wanted to go outside and tell the people out there what had happened, or at least feed them the lies she had sworn to repeat, but she could not move. She just stared into her father's dead eyes as he lay before her, thankful that her brother and sisters were still upstairs, asleep.

'This is the house, here,' she heard someone say.

There was a knock at the door, and another voice called, 'Hello!'

She heard the front door open. She supposed her mother must have left it ajar in her haste to leave.

'Hello?' the voice said again, inside the house now. 'Mr Bates? Mrs Bates? Is anyone home?'

Jess stirred at last, wondering who was there. Her eyes flashed to the open doorway and she saw a policeman in his uniform. The sight of him confused her at first.

How could the authorities already have known about her father and Mr Butterfill? She wanted to say something, anything, but as she tried to speak she found that her throat was too dry and she coughed instead.

'Oh my good Lord!' the policeman said when he saw the bodies. 'What on earth's happened here then?' Clearly, he knew nothing about this at all. How then did he come to be there? His eyes now on Jess, he added, 'Are you all right, miss?'

Jess nodded, although she wasn't entirely sure that she was all right. Why was she still trembling so, and why could she not stand up?

'Don't trouble yourself, miss,' the policeman said, clearly having seen the difficulty she was having as she tried to get to her feet. 'You stay right there while I fetch some help.'

With that, the policeman ran outside and started blowing his whistle. A moment later someone else replaced him. Ephraim Black was standing in the doorway, holding up a small oil lamp.

'Jess?' he said, his eyes flitting from her to the two dead bodies on the floor. 'You poor thing.' He put the lamp down and went to her, mindful of where he stepped. 'Here, let me help you up.'

Very slowly, Jess took his hand, and Ephraim helped her to her feet. He took off his coat and wrapped it around her shoulders.

'Where is your mother?' Ephraim asked.

'Gone,' Jess said. 'She's run off and wants nothing more to do with us. How did you know where to find me?' She was certain she had never told him where she lived, out of fear he might bring her back again.

'When your father brought you home,' Ephraim said,

'I followed after you, just as he had had someone follow you to my house. I was worried about you, because of what your father might do to you when he got you home, and because of what you told me, about the man you were to marry.'

'That's him there,' Jess said, pointing down at Butterfill's grey-faced corpse.

Ephraim looked at him. He put his arms around Jess's shoulders. 'You should never have to see such things,' he said. 'Now, let's get you out of here.'

Ephraim led Jess around the room, away from the bodies. He collected his lamp again, and as they arrived at the front door, another policeman joined the first. One of them went inside, the other remained with her.

'Can you tell us what happened, miss?' the policeman asked. 'If it's not too soon to talk about it, that is?'

'Can it wait until the morning, officer?' Ephraim said. 'The poor girl needs to rest.'

Before the policeman could answer, Jess spoke. 'It's all right. I'd sooner get it over and done with.' Then she repeated what the Fuller brothers wanted her to say. 'Mr Butterfill came to collect the rent, only my dad couldn't pay him,' she lied, never once looking at Ephraim, having vowed never to lie to him again. 'They got into a row, and suddenly my dad had Mr Butterfill up against the wall. Then Mr Butterfill took a knife out of his pocket and stabbed him.'

'Mr Butterfill stabbed your dad?' the policeman repeated.

'That's right, but then my dad took the knife off Mr Butterfill and he cut his throat with it. Then they both fell down, dead. Mum couldn't take it any more. She's run off.'

'I see,' the policeman said, scratching at his chin. 'A nasty business.'

Upstairs, the twins began to cry, no doubt having been disturbed at last by the sound of the policeman's whistle.

'My brother and my sisters are up in the back room,' Jess said. 'They don't know nothing about it.'

Ephraim's eyes wandered up the narrow staircase. 'Perhaps we had better go up and sit with them for a while.'

'That's a good idea,' the policeman said.

'What'll happen to us?' Jess asked as they went.

'Well, you still have a home with Stephen and me, if you wish.'

'What about Hannah and Charlie, and the twins?'

'As much as I'd like to, I'm afraid I can't take you all in,' Ephraim said. 'Without my dear wife at my side, I very much doubt I could give them the upbringing they deserve, and I have Stephen to think of. He's taken to you, but as I've said, that is a very rare thing indeed.'

They reached the top of the stairs and Jess stopped. Then, in a whisper so that Hannah and Charlie could not hear her, she said, 'I can't live with you if they're for the workhouse.'

'The workhouse?' Ephraim repeated. 'Good lord, I'm sure we can find them better homes than that!'

'You promise?'

'Yes, I promise,' Ephraim said. 'I'll see to it personally that they're all well placed, and that you'll be able to go and see them whenever you like.'

'And they'll be able to come and see me?'

Ephraim smiled. 'Yes, of course,' he said. 'These things I promise you with all my heart.' He held his lamp up and gestured to the back-room door. 'Now, perhaps you would like to introduce us.'

Jess returned Ephraim's smile, thinking that because of him things would perhaps turn out the better for all of them. As she turned the doorknob and they stepped inside the room, she wondered what she had done to deserve her chance encounter with Ephraim Black, and above all, his friendship. He owed her nothing, and yet he had promised her everything she could ever have wished for.

CHAPTER TWENTY-FIVE

Present day

Following their conversation with Inspector Dalton, Tayte and Nat returned to Ravenscourt Park to see what Felicity Greenwood had found in her attic. She had not said much during her brief telephone conversation with Tayte, but what she did say had piqued his interest. She had found the astronomy journals she'd mentioned on their previous visit, and said she thought that one of them would be of particular interest. It was late morning by the time they arrived. No biscuits were served with the tea this time. Instead, as Felicity was expecting them on this occasion, she had a Victoria sponge waiting. They sat in the sitting room around the glass coffee table as before.

'I'm afraid I didn't have time to make the cake myself,' she said when she noticed Tayte staring at it. 'So I popped out to the shops right after our phone call.'

'You shouldn't have gone to such bother, Mrs Greenwood,' Tayte said. 'But thank you.'

Felicity cut him a big slice and handed it to him with a smile. She turned to Nat. 'Would you like some, dear?'

'Thank you,' Nat said. 'Just a small piece.'

Felicity cut into the cake again. 'Any news from the police about your painting?' she asked as she handed the slice to Nat.

'Not yet, Mrs Greenwood, but I'm hopeful.'

Felicity smiled again. 'That's the spirit,' she said, and they all settled back with their tea and their cake.

Tayte tried a piece. 'It's very nice,' he said. 'Are you going out for Sunday lunch today?' he added, noticing how smartly dressed she was, in a fitted navy-blue dress and heels, drop earrings, and a heavy gold chain at her neck.

'No, not this weekend,' Felicity said, contradicting his thoughts. 'Today, it's just me, myself and I.'

Like the cake, Tayte thought she must have gone to the bother just because she knew she was having company. But what did he know? Maybe she was in the habit of dressing up on Sundays. The 'Sunday best' wasn't just for church these days. He took another bite of his cake and set it down on the coffee table. As he did so, he noticed something on the shelf beneath the tabletop. He thought it must be the journal he and Nat had gone there to see. He craned his head around to get a better look at it. There was a picture of a meteorite on the front cover, hurtling through space.

'Of course!' Felicity said, sitting forward as she saw Tayte looking at the journal. She put her teacup down. 'You're not here for the tea and cake, are you?' She reached down and lifted the journal out. She read the title aloud. *'Journal of the British Astronomical Association,'* she said. 'Volume 30. October 1919 to September 1920.' She handed it to Tayte. 'One of the pages has a corner folded over. I think you'll find it very interesting.'

Tayte took the journal from her and sat closer to Nat so she could also see it. He opened it to the page someone had singled out, suspecting the corner had been folded over some time ago as the crease had yellowed with age.

'It was in the trunk,' Felicity said. 'I knew I'd seen the name Jess, or Jessie in this case, before. It was a few years ago now. When I came across the journal, I couldn't resist taking a look at the page that had been marked.'

'Was there anything else in there you think might be of interest?' Tayte asked.

'No. Just rubbish really. I must get around to clearing it all out.'

Tayte and Nat studied the journal page together. A moment later, Nat tapped a bright-green fingernail on the name Jessie Chilcott.

'Chilcott,' Tayte mused as he read it, wondering whether this was the Jessie they were interested in.

He studied the page. It was a thesis on 'Island universes'. Further reading told him that it challenged the belief that objects in space, known at the time as nebulae, were gas clouds in the Milky Way, suggesting that they were not part of our galaxy at all, but were actually more distant galaxies in themselves. He turned a few pages and saw that the piece was several pages long.

'At this time, Jessie Chilcott could be just about anyone,' he said, thinking aloud as he took out his phone and photographed the page. 'Although we have to wonder why this journal was in a trunk that belongs to this family, and why this page in particular has been singled out.'

'I suspect Ephraim might have marked it,' Felicity said. 'I'm sure they would have belonged to him as the astronomer in the family.'

Nat put her cake down. 'Do you think she could be the

Jess in my painting?' she asked Tayte.

'I think it's highly likely,' Tayte said. 'Ephraim appears to have taken particular interest in the piece – perhaps even pride, if Jessie Chilcott here was, as I suspect, his protégé. Chilcott could be her married name. The records will tell us whether or not her maiden name is Black.'

'His daughter?' Nat said. 'So this is the adoption we've been looking for.'

Tayte nodded. 'At least, that's what I think we're going to find. Now that we have some other names to work with, I also believe we'll be able to prove it.'

Nat was beaming, and Tayte could see that she was as keen as he was to get on and do just that. She was finishing her cake, already half out of her seat.

'Thank you, Felicity,' Tayte said as he handed the journal back to her. 'You've given us a key piece of the puzzle we're trying to unravel.'

'Glad to have been of service,' Felicity said. 'It's all been rather exciting for me, to be honest.'

Tayte leaned forward and took another forkful of his cake. He quickly washed it down with what was left of his tea and stood up. 'Before we go,' he said, 'your brother Geoffrey said some odd things when we went to see him yesterday.'

'Did he?' Felicity said. 'Such as?'

'He told us his wife was unwell – that she suffered with migraines. He's not married, though, is he?'

'Not to my knowledge. How curious.'

'You've no idea why he might have said that then?'

'None whatsoever,' Felicity said. She laughed. 'Perhaps he's lost his marbles and invented one for company. I'm afraid I really couldn't say.'

Tayte threw her a smile. 'Well, we won't take up any more of your time,' he said. 'Thanks again for helping us, and for your hospitality.'

CHAPTER TWENTY-SIX

Back at the Marcus Brown School of Family History, Tayte and Nat both pulled out their laptops and set up at the desk.

'So, what do we know for a fact?' Tayte asked as he began logging in to some of his family history subscription services.

Nat pulled a face and stared at the ceiling. A moment later, she said, 'Not much really, I suppose.'

'What do you mean?' Tayte said. 'We know plenty.'

'We do?'

Tayte nodded. 'We know the painting of Jess was made in 1891, so she clearly knew Stephen Black by then. The census, taken in April that year, shows Jessie Bates living with her parents and siblings at an address in Pottery Lane, North Kensington. Those are the facts you came to me with. Now, today we have a connection in an astronomy journal between the Black family we're interested in, via the astronomer Ephraim Black, and someone called Jessie Chilcott. From those facts, I believe she took that name through marriage, and that prior to that she was called Jessie Black.'

'Adopted into the Black family,' Nat said.

'Exactly. It's got to be the adoption we're looking for. That art expert, Huckabee, was technically correct when he said that Stephen Black was the only child of Ephraim and Eudora Black, but that didn't mean there wasn't another child in the family, not of their making – an adopted child.'

'But we still have to prove it.'

'Yes, we do,' Tayte said. 'That part is still a theory at this time, based on what we have.' He smiled to himself. 'It's no wonder you hit a brick wall.'

'So what's the next step?'

'Well, as I said before, we're unlikely to find an adoption record for Jess, and you've already tried. I do believe, however, that we're just three records away from proving unequivocal probability, which is the next best thing in this game. Let's take a look at the 1901 census. Do you want to bring that up while I access the birth, marriage and death indexes? See if you can find Ephraim Black. There shouldn't be too many results for a name like that. With everything we've learned, if Jessie Bates was adopted into the Black family sometime after 1891, I wouldn't mind betting we'll find her living under the same roof in 1901.'

Nat accessed the 1901 census and entered Ephraim Black's name into the search fields. Tayte brought up the birth, marriage and death index website he liked to use and did the same for Jessie Chilcott.

'I want to see if I can find a marriage record for a Jessie Black, who married a man named Chilcott,' he said as he typed. 'If we are on the right track, it should exist.'

They each tapped away at their keyboards, digging into the archives. Nat was first to get a result.

'Here it is,' she said. 'Ephraim John Black is shown as

the head of the household. There's no wife listed, so I suppose she must have died or otherwise left him by then, and he hadn't remarried. Stephen Ebenezer Black's relationship to the head of the household is shown as son, confirming I have the right record.' She paused, and her face flushed with excitement as she added, 'And here's Jessie Black – no middle name. Her relationship to the head of the household is shown as daughter.'

Tayte slid his chair alongside her so he could take a look at her screen to see the entry for himself. 'There she is,' he said, in no doubt that this had to be Jessie Bates. How else might Stephen Black's painting of 'Jess' have wound up in Nat's family – Nat, who was descended from Jessie Bates's brother, Charlie? It was a good start, but he knew the remaining records he wanted to look at could increase the probability further. He slid his chair back to his laptop.

'Take a look at this,' he said. 'I think I'm close to finding a record of marriage for Jess.'

Nat inched closer to Tayte as he finished his search. On his screen was a list of those people called Jessie Black who had matched his search criteria. There were several, but not many for London districts, in one of which Tayte imagined Jess would have been married. He had already gone through a few of them, with no mention of the name Chilcott so far. There were only two left, though, and he was confident it had to be one of them. He opened the next one and clicked on the button to view the original index entry. A moment later he was presented with a scan of the original index page for marriages registered in October, November and December 1915, which contained the entry he was looking for.

'There,' he said, pointing it out to Nat as soon as he

saw it. 'Black, Jessie.' He traced his finger across to the other surname. 'And there's Chilcott.'

'She married quite late, didn't she?' Nat said. 'Late for those times, at least. She would have been thirty-six.'

'Perhaps her studies in the field of astronomy kept her mind off boys up until then,' Tayte offered. 'Who knows? Maybe it just took a while for Mr Right to come along. It's a good thing for us, though, or we might have had to wait on a certificate from the General Register Office. The spouse's name is only shown on the indexes from 1912.'

Just the same, Tayte noted down the district, volume and page number, so he could later order a copy of the certificate to verify his findings. For now, however, he was confident that the index had told them everything they needed to know – that the maiden name of Jessie Chilcott, whose thesis they had read about in the 1919-1920 British Astronomical Association journal they had seen, was Black.

'That's pretty conclusive then,' Nat said. 'Jess was adopted into the Black family, became a respected amateur astronomer, like her adoptive father, Ephraim, and later married someone called Chilcott.' She fixed on Tayte with a puzzled expression. 'You said we were three records away from as good as proving all this. What's the third? Why do we need any more than this?'

'What we have so far is pretty good,' Tayte said. 'You're right in that it tells us all the things you just mentioned, but so far the only thing telling us that Jessie Black is Jessie Bates is the fact that your painting by Stephen Black of a girl called "Jess" has been in your Bates family for a while. The connection is there. You could be happy with that and move on, but there's one more record to find, which could increase the probability exponentially.'

Tayte gave Nat an expectant look, hoping she was about to furnish him with the answer. He was really getting into this teaching thing. He could see she was thinking about it. He'd give her a while longer. Twenty seconds later, he gave her a clue.

'It's linked to one of the three main types of family history records genealogists use.'

'Death records?' Nat said, as if questioning herself.

'Are you just guessing, or do you know where you're going with that?'

Nat smiled. 'I know,' she said, more confidently. 'Linked to death records are the records of a person's last will and testament. People typically mention other family members in their wills. Maybe our Jessie Chilcott left something to one of her Bates siblings. Perhaps even my painting.'

'Bravo!' Tayte said. He clapped his hands, applauding her until her cheeks became as red as the streaks in her hair. 'That's a perfect piece of genealogical deduction right there. A person's will can be a gold mine of information.'

Tayte turned his attention back to his laptop. 'First, we need to know when Jessie Chilcott died.' He went back to his birth, marriage and death index search and entered Jessie Chilcott into the search fields, opting to look at deaths only this time. Just a few results came back. He soon found the entry he was looking for. It correlated with Jessie Bates's year of birth, giving him confidence that he was looking at the right entry. It was listed on the index under deaths registered in January, February and March 1961.

'She lived to the age of eighty-one,' Tayte said as he

noted down the details from the index entry. 'As it's Sunday, we're not going to be able to see a copy of Jess's will anytime today,' he added. 'I have some contacts at the General Register Office, though. I'll call tomorrow and see if I can speed things up a little. They should be able to send me a digital copy by the end of the day.'

'That's a pity,' Nat said. 'Shame it's not a weekday.'

Tayte laughed. She seemed more impatient to see the record than he was. 'It's only tomorrow.'

'I guess we'll just have to wait then,' she said. 'So that's it for today?'

'It's been a good day,' Tayte reminded her.

'Yes, it has.'

Nat went quiet and began to flick at her lip stud. Tayte had noticed she often did that when she wanted to say something but couldn't seem to find the words, or was nervous about voicing them. He knew something was on her mind.

'What is it?' he asked her. 'What's troubling you?'

Nat let out a sigh. 'I want to go back and ask Geoffrey Black why he lied to us,' she said. 'We've as good as solved my brick wall and proved who the girl in the painting is or was, and we've learned a lot about her along the way, but someone killed my cousin and stole my painting. Like you, I think Geoffrey Black knows something about it and I'd like to find out what.'

'I was hoping you'd feel that way,' Tayte said. He checked his watch. 'I guess I can't let you go by yourself, though, can I?' he added, closing his laptop. 'It's not much after four. Let's go and shake the tree together – see what falls out.'

CHAPTER TWENTY-SEVEN

When Tayte and Nat arrived back at Geoffrey Black's house in Putney, Tayte's eyes were immediately drawn to the car that was parked outside.

'Isn't that Felicity Greenwood's car?' he said, indicating the silver, all-electric Jaguar that seemed identical to the one he'd seen each time they went to see her.

Nat looked it over. 'I didn't take note of the registration number,' she said, 'but it looks the same.'

Tayte rang the doorbell. A moment later, Geoffrey Black answered. He looked surprised to see them back on his doorstep.

'Mr Black,' Tayte said. 'I'm sorry to trouble you again, but something's been bothering us since we came to see you yesterday, and I was hoping you could help clear it up for us.'

'I have nothing further to say to you,' Black said. 'Now please leave.'

He began to close the door.

'You mentioned the name Jess before either of us did, Mr Black,' Tayte persisted. 'We'd just like to know how you already knew that name.'

Black paused, the door still ajar. 'I must have heard it

on that TV news report, in connection with the painting you were talking about.'

Through the gap in the door, Tayte noticed that Geoffrey kept looking behind him, as though someone else was there. 'That's just the thing,' Tayte said. 'Jess's name was never mentioned in that news report.'

'Then you must have said it first when you came to see me yesterday,' Black said, just as Inspector Dalton had told them he would. 'Now please go away!'

Tayte wasn't ready to give up just yet. Geoffrey Black had lied to them and he and Nat wanted to know why. 'Then how about your wife?' he said. 'You don't have one, do you? Why did you lie to us about that?'

The door opened further then, but it was not Geoffrey Black who opened it. It was Felicity Greenwood. Being the more amicable of the two, she was smiling as usual. 'Step aside, Geoffrey,' she told him. 'Let's not keep your visitors talking on the doorstep.' To Tayte and Nat, she added, 'I'm sorry. Do come in, won't you? I'm sure we can straighten all this out in no time over a hot cup of tea.'

Tayte thought Geoffrey looked decidedly troubled now, as he and Nat took up Felicity's invitation and entered the house. He thought he'd be worried, too, under the circumstances. If Geoffrey did know something about Jess, then Tayte could only imagine it had to be in connection with the stolen painting, and the murder of Nat's cousin. They followed Felicity into the sitting room while Geoffrey tagged along behind them.

'Go and put the kettle on, Geoffrey,' Felicity said as she, Tayte and Nat sat down.

They were seated on a tired brown three-piece suite, around a tatty old gas fire that seemed a poor choice of focal point. Unlike Felicity's house, the decor here was stuck in the 1970s, with beige and brown circular patterned wallpaper, worn teak wooden furniture, and a clutter of random ornaments that put Tayte in mind of a bric-a-brac store. At the end of the room, opposite the window that faced the street, was a set of double doors with obscure patterned glass. As soon as Geoffrey disappeared through them to make the tea, Felicity started talking.

'Geoffrey has problems,' she said, keeping her voice down. 'I didn't like to say before, when you told me he said his wife was unwell, but I suppose now is the time.'

'What kind of problems?' Nat asked.

'How can I put this delicately?' Felicity said with a sigh. 'Geoffrey is socially awkward. More specifically, he suffers from social anxiety disorder. He doesn't like being around people. He fears their rejection, and that he's being judged all the time. He deals with it by choosing to avoid social contact wherever he can.'

'So he lied to us about his wife,' Nat said, 'as a reason to make us go away?'

'Precisely,' Felicity said. 'We believe his mental disorder harks back to our artist ancestor, Stephen Black. Did you know he was autistic?'

'Yes, we did,' Nat said. 'An art expert we went to see about my stolen painting filled us in on a few things.'

'Well, there you have it,' Felicity said. 'Mental disorders seem to run in the Black family.'

Tayte thought Felicity's explanation was entirely plausible. He also thought that Felicity had had plenty of time to come up with that answer, given that he'd posed the question to her at her house a couple of hours earlier. Maybe, as Geoffrey's sister, she was trying to protect him.

'That doesn't explain how he knew Jess's name before

I told him,' Tayte said.

'Perhaps you really were mistaken, Mr Tayte,' Felicity said. 'It's so easy to slip a name into a conversation here and there and think nothing of it. I seem to recall your friend here mentioning Jess's name to me quite early on when you first visited.'

Tayte was getting tired of people challenging his memory. If he wasn't sure about something, he'd be the first to admit it, but he knew he was right about this. Jess's name was in Geoffrey Black's mind long before he and Nat showed up on his doorstep.

The double doors opened and Geoffrey brought in the tea. Without saying a word, or looking at anyone, he handed everyone a cup and put the tray with the milk and sugar down on top of a low footstool that didn't seem very stable.

'I was just telling our guests about your social anxiety disorder, Geoffrey,' Felicity said. 'I've explained that you don't like being around people. That's why you made up the story about your pretend wife, so you didn't have to talk to them any longer than you had to.'

Geoffrey stared at Felicity for a moment. Then he stirred some sugar into his tea and sat down.

'They're still a little confused about this Jess thing,' Felicity continued. 'Is there anywhere you might have seen the name, and as a consequence known whom Mr Tayte and his friend were talking about?'

Geoffrey began to shake his head.

'You must have gone through that trunk in the attic after Daddy died,' Felicity said. 'Could that be it? Surely that's how you knew her name, as I did, from one of our ancestor's astronomy journals.' She turned to Tayte. 'There you have it, Mr Tayte. Geoffrey has simply put two and two together. He may be socially awkward, but like Stephen's, his mind is as bright as a new penny.'

Tayte scoffed. It had seemingly all been resolved and Geoffrey hadn't spoken a word. He wasn't buying any of it. 'Mrs Greenwood, are you trying to protect your brother from something?' It was an accusatory thing to say, but Tayte couldn't help himself. It just came out.

It was Geoffrey who answered. 'No, she is not!' he said, sounding very adamant about it. 'And neither do I suffer from any social anxiety disorder.'

Just then, Tayte noticed a tall shadow move across the obscure glass doors at the end of the room. 'Who else is here?' he asked, confused as to why their presence had not been mentioned. He had the feeling that whoever it was had been hiding in the kitchen all along for some reason.

Geoffrey sighed. 'It's my brothers,' he said. 'Come out, come out, wherever you are!' he called. 'Our guests have rumbled you.'

'Geoffrey!' Felicity said. 'Whatever's got into you?'

'Frankly, the lot of you have,' Geoffrey said. 'I wish you'd all leave. I told you I wanted no part in this.'

Tayte was about to ask Geoffrey exactly what it was that he wanted no part in. He could guess well enough, but now Geoffrey's resolve to keep quiet appeared to be crumbling, and Tayte wanted to hear it from him. At the far end of the room, however, the double doors opened and two men walked in from the kitchen, distracting him. He recognised Brendan Black from the fine art prints shop he and Nat had visited. He was wearing the same grey pinstripe, three-piece suit he'd been wearing when they first met. The other man, a burly-looking man in blue jeans and a grey polo shirt, Tayte did not recognise, but he knew he had to be Lawrence Black, the brother who had been reluctant to answer his front door when they tried to speak with him previously. Neither man was smiling – quite the opposite.

Without knowing exactly why, Tayte felt threatened by their approach. He stood up. 'I thought you said you didn't keep in touch with the rest of your family,' he said to Brendan, maintaining a confident tone, yet beginning to feel anything but. 'Just cards at Christmas, wasn't it?' he added. 'But here you all are.' He turned to Felicity. 'Would you care to explain what's going on here?'

For once, Felicity was lost for words.

'What is it you wanted no part in, Geoffrey?' Tayte asked him. His eyes drifted down to Nat. She looked as afraid now as he was to hear the answer.

'Don't say a word, Geoffrey!' Felicity barked at him.

At the same time, Tayte noticed Lawrence shake his head, as though warning Geoffrey to keep his mouth shut. Looking back at Geoffrey, Tayte could see his hands were shaking.

'I can't keep quiet about this any longer,' Geoffrey said. 'My nerves can't take it. It has to stop right now!'

'Geoffrey,' Brendan now warned.

Geoffrey wasn't listening. He turned to face Felicity, and as if they were the only two people in the room, he said, 'You and your grand ideas! We'll all get rich, you said, and why shouldn't we profit from our ancestor's success? Well, now someone's dead.'

Tayte felt the blood drain from his cheeks. He knew at once that Geoffrey's words had put him and Nat in great danger. They hadn't gone back there expecting to hear Geoffrey Black spill the proverbial beans on the rest of his family, but the pressure of keeping quiet about it, no doubt afraid that he might be implicated in not just an art theft, but murder, had finally got to him. Tayte supposed that that was why Felicity had gone there that afternoon, and why she had called her other brothers there, too. After Tayte and Nat's visit with Felicity earlier that day, she had become concerned about Geoffrey and what he might say. She had called a family meeting. Now it had all imploded, and Tayte and Nat were caught in the middle.

'Well, thanks for clearing that up,' Tayte said, forcing a bright tone as he spoke, as if to suggest that everything was just fine. He quickly pulled Nat to her feet. 'We'll just be on our way now.'

Tayte hadn't expected to get out of there that easily, not after everything he and Nat had heard. He wasn't wrong. He caught a sharp look from Felicity, but it wasn't aimed at him. It was directed at Lawrence. As Tayte turned towards him, he saw a heavy-looking glass vase briefly before it crashed into the side of his head. He was momentarily aware of pain and of falling.

Then nothing.

CHAPTER TWENTY-EIGHT

When Jefferson Tayte regained consciousness, the first thoughts to enter his head concerned Nat. Where was she? Was she all right? His eyes flickered open and he saw her beside him, bound and gagged as he was, her wide eyes staring into his. He was aware then of something in one of his eyes, causing him to blink. It was blood – his blood, from the blow he'd just received. It had run down from the side of his head where the vase had struck him, and was now all over his jacket. As he became fully conscious again, his heart began to pound. He tried to communicate with Nat. He nodded his head in the hope that she would nod back at him, but all he got from her was that same wide-eyed stare. Even without the gag at his mouth, what could he tell her? No one knew they were there. Who else could help them but themselves? It was a despairing thought because he knew they were in no position to do so.

Tayte had faced situations like this before. He'd had guns pointed at his head, and had even faced torture as a result of digging up past lives that others in the present day would rather remain buried. He still felt afraid of what was going to happen to them next, however, and he could only imagine how Nat was feeling. They were tied at their wrists and above their knees with belts and colourful neckties – things that came easily to hand in the home. Opposite them, in one of the armchairs, Geoffrey was also bound and gagged. The other three were standing by the fireplace.

Brendan's face looked flushed, as though he'd been the one running about the house finding things to tie them up with. 'This is all getting a bit out of hand,' he said. 'What are we going to do with them?'

Lawrence was staring at the side of Tayte's head, as if admiring his handiwork. 'We can't just let them go, can we?' he said. 'Not now.'

'No,' Brendan said. 'Not now that you've bloody well knocked one of them senseless!'

'They'd heard too much,' Lawrence said. He turned away, his eyes now on Geoffrey. 'All thanks to him.'

Felicity spoke then. 'Stop squabbling, the pair of you. We don't have to do anything hasty. They can't stay here, of course. We must move them – give ourselves time to think.'

'I've got my van outside,' Lawrence said. 'I know some people who could babysit them for a bit. They're the kind of people who could even take care of them for us for a price, if you catch my drift.'

Tayte caught it full on. He began to shake his head. He wanted to tell them that they didn't have to do this – that the charges against them would be more lenient if they let them go. They would be charged with theft and murder, yes, but the murder of Nat's cousin had surely been unintentional. Killing them now, or having them killed, was premeditated murder in the first degree. He wanted to say all that, knowing it would likely fall on deaf ears anyway, but the gag at his mouth prevented him.

Geoffrey began to squeal through his gag. He tried to stand up, clearly in a state of utter panic over the situation he also now found himself in. He was quickly shoved back down into his seat.

'You keep quiet!' Lawrence said, pointing a warning finger at him. 'This is your fault. If you'd come in with the rest of us, none of this would be happening now.'

'We can't have Geoffrey killed,' Brendan said, voicing the darkest of their options. 'He's our brother, for Christ's sake.'

'Leave him here,' Felicity said. 'We'll deal with him later.' Directly to Lawrence, she added, 'Is your van parked far away?'

'It's down the road a bit.'

'Go and fetch it. Bring it to the front of the house and leave the engine running.'

Lawrence was quick to go, and Tayte was glad to see the back of him. With just Brendan and Felicity there now, he thought he had a better chance of improving the situation, but how? With the gag at his mouth, he could hardly talk himself out of this one. He knew he didn't have long to think about it, so he quickly concluded that the best option, possibly the only option under the circumstances, was to try to make it out of the house. Maybe someone would see him, bound and gagged, and would raise the alarm. He looked at Nat again and knew instantly that, whatever he was going to do, he had to do it by himself. She looked rigid with fear, and even if she was able to do anything, he had no way of communicating his intentions to her.

Felicity was pacing back and forth at the window,

looking out for Lawrence's van. Brendan was keeping watch in front of them. It was one on one, and although Tayte had the disadvantage of being bound, he was the heavier man by far. The front door wasn't far away. If Tayte had had the time to think about what he did next, he might have quickly talked himself out of it. As it was, as soon as Brendan took his eyes off them, he rocked himself back into the sofa cushion and then sprang to his feet, knocking Brendan flying.

Without looking to see how effective his assault had been, Tayte hobbled around the sofa and headed as quickly as he could for the door. His progress was painfully slow, like being caught in a nightmare he couldn't escape from. He made it all the way to the hallway, in sight of the front door, before he felt a hand grab at his arm. He spun around and saw that it was Felicity. Instead of continuing for the door, he shoved her with his shoulder, knocking her back. A moment later he was awkwardly turning the door catch, cursing the necktie that had been used to bind his wrists. The door swung open and he began to hobble along the path outside, yelling into his gag. Then he saw a white van pull up beyond the gate. He had nowhere to go. He looked around, but there was no one else out there.

Lawrence saw Tayte at once. He shot out of his van and came hurtling along the path with the determination of a rugby player heading for the goal line. He bowled into Tayte just as Brendan caught up with him. Then, instead of taking Tayte back inside the house, as Tayte had now done half the work for them, they pulled and pushed him along the path and out through the gate. In no time at all, Tayte found himself inside the back of Lawrence Black's van.

'Get the girl!' Lawrence barked, clearly annoyed that he'd only stepped out for a few minutes and had returned to see Tayte escaping. 'You think you can handle that?'

'There's no need for your sarcasm,' Brendan said.

Tayte heard Felicity then. Her words brought him hope.

'She's gone!' Felicity called. 'The kitchen door wasn't locked. She's slipped out the back.'

'Christ!' Lawrence said.

Tayte had noticed there was a side gate to the right of the house, giving access to the back. He imagined that Nat, having found no way out of the garden she'd escaped into, had come around the front, trying to make it to the road, as he had. He heard a car coming then, but it quickly passed without stopping. A moment later, his hopes were shattered.

'There she is!' Brendan called out.

'Then bloody well get after her!' Lawrence said.

It fell quiet. Tayte wished it were any other day than Sunday or there might have been more traffic around – more people out and about in this quiet little conservation area of Putney. His heart sank when the doors to the back of the van opened and Nat was none too delicately shoved in beside him. Before the doors closed, however, Tayte heard another car, and then another, and this time they both came to a tyre-squealing stop right beside the van, hemming it in. Tayte heard car doors being opened. Then people began shouting – people other than the Black family.

'Police!' someone yelled, and it was the most welcome word Tayte could have hoped to hear.

He thought Inspector Dalton must have had the house watched – perhaps all of their houses – in case one of the

Black family had the painting and tried to move it. Or perhaps Dalton's suspicions of Geoffrey Black, who, as it turned out, appeared to be the only innocent member of the Black family, had been piqued by their recent conversation and he had put close surveillance on the man. Whatever the reason, Tayte was thankful.

CHAPTER TWENTY-NINE

Exactly one week after Tayte first met Nat, when she had shown him her photograph of the girl in the painting and introduced him to her genealogical brick wall, he was standing in front of a class again, giving eight enthusiastic students his closing tips for the day. This time, however, he did so with a bruised lump on the side of his head and several butterfly stitches.

'And remember,' he said as the students began to leave, 'not only should you be in the habit of citing your sources, but you should also be sure to verify them whenever possible.'

It was another of Tayte's rules not to assume anything when it came to genealogical research, but there were exceptions, especially if that assumption was being used to prove a theory or gut feeling about something, as had been the case with Jessie Bates's adoption into the Black family.

He threw a wink at Nat, who was still sitting at her foldaway desk, looking as colourful as ever in a loose-fitting, rainbow-patterned jumper, waiting to see him after class. He was glad to see that their recent ordeal hadn't dampened her spirits too much or put her off genealogy for good. Such things were a big part of why he'd become a teacher, and this was a good reminder for him to stay behind his desk. He just couldn't help himself, and yet again, here was proof of that. He always seemed to be drawn to those assignments that involved murder.

As the last of his students drifted out, Tayte saw the reason Nat was staying behind that evening. Inspector Dalton was there in his dark suit and tie, once more filling the classroom door frame. Tayte beckoned him in, prompting Nat to stand up as the inspector approached.

'Thanks for sticking around to see me,' Dalton said. 'I think you'll find it worthwhile.'

'Did you get a confession?' Tayte asked.

'Eventually, yes. Geoffrey Black was very talkative. The others were tight-lipped for a while, but they knew this was only going to end one way.'

'Is Geoffrey being charged?'

'That seems unlikely at this time. It appears he was the only one of the Black family who wanted nothing to do with it. The others all played their role, though. The mastermind, the thief and the fence.'

'And the murderer,' Nat added.

'Yes, of course – and the murderer. That was Lawrence Black. Felicity planned the whole thing after she found a notebook in a trunk in her attic. It contained a catalogue of paintings by their artist ancestor, Stephen Ebenezer Black.'

'She never told us about that,' Nat said to Tayte.

'No, she didn't,' Tayte said. 'She knew it would incriminate her.'

Dalton turned to Nat. 'One of the entries in the catalogue was for your painting called "Jess", Miss Cooper. It turns out Felicity had been following the sale of these paintings for some years, trying to get her hands on one or more of them, but the price kept rising, further and further out of her reach. Over time, she managed to account for nearly all of S E Black's works, through one auction and another, but "Jess" remained a mystery. She began to imagine what might have come of it. She conducted some genealogical research of her own and found out who Jess was. Then, via Jess's brother, Charlie Bates, she found your family, Miss Cooper.'

'How did they plan to sell the painting?' Tayte asked.

'That's where Brendan Black comes in,' Dalton said. 'Through his business, he's established plenty of contacts in the art world, and not all of them legit.'

'Did they tell you where the painting is?' Nat asked. 'Do they still have it?'

Dalton nodded. 'It was at Felicity Greenwood's house. Now it's safe and sound in police custody. You'll get it back in due course, Miss Cooper, but you understand that we have to hold it as evidence for the time being.'

'Of course,' Nat said.

'What will you do with it?' Tayte asked her, knowing it wasn't such an easy question to answer, given the painting's value.

'I don't know,' Nat said. 'I couldn't afford to insure it, and I'd be forever wondering if anyone else was trying to break in to steal it. I'd probably never get a good night's sleep again. I think I'll put it up for auction, but it feels wrong to make money from it, given what's happened. I'll give a large portion of the proceeds to my late cousin's family, and the rest to Trisha's favourite charity, in her name. Perhaps they'll put a plaque up or name something after her so she won't be forgotten.'

'I'm sure she would have liked that very much,' Tayte

said.

Nat gave a sombre smile and nodded, her thoughts having turned to the true remaining victim in all this.

'Well,' Dalton said. 'I'll leave you both to it for now. I'll be in touch regarding the trial proceedings. In the meantime, if there's anything you need from me, just let me or one of my team know.' He turned to go. 'And thank you both,' he added. 'I never expected this to turn out the way it did, and I'm glad you're both okay, but it's because of you and what you've done that the people responsible for your cousin's death, Miss Cooper, are going to pay for what they did.'

They watched in silence as Dalton left and their parting, cheerless smiles began to wane. Once he'd gone, Tayte turned to Nat and said, 'I have something for you.'

Tayte pulled his briefcase up on to his desk and opened it. He drew out a plain Manila folder and handed it to Nat. 'It's a copy of Jessie Chilcott's last will and testament.'

Nat opened the folder and began to read the document. 'Looks like she died a wealthy woman,' she said a moment later. 'Along with her estate, it mentions the rights to several books about astronomy, too.' She paused, smiling to herself. 'From what I know, she did better for herself than my great-great-grandfather, Charlie.'

'Perhaps she had more encouragement,' Tayte said, 'and don't forget opportunity. Jess was obviously a highly intelligent girl. Her adoption by Ephraim Black allowed for that intelligence to be nurtured.'

'So, we know for sure that she was adopted?'

'Read on,' Tayte said.

Jess kept reading. 'It shows she left most of her estate

to her two children, and she had plenty of friends, by the look of it.' She paused. 'It mentions four other children here, too.'

Tayte smiled. 'So it does,' he said, knowing that she was about to realise she was looking at the final piece of proof he was hoping to find.

'There's the twins, Emma and Lillian,' Nat said. 'And there's Hannah and Charlie.' She paused, her face suddenly beaming. 'She left her portrait to him – my painting.'

'Yes, she did,' Tayte said. 'I suspect that's how Felicity Greenwood knew where it might be found today. Inspector Dalton just told us she'd been tracking down the pieces that had been sold over the years. It stands to reason that if this never had been sold, there was a good chance it was still in your great-great-grandfather's family.'

'I wonder why Jess left it to Charlie at all,' Nat said. 'Rather than leaving it to one of her children, I mean.'

'Who knows what guides decisions like that?' Tayte said. 'It was 1961, and no doubt earlier than that when the will was drawn up. From what we've heard about the rise in S E Black's popularity, back then the painting wouldn't have been worth anything like as much as it is today. Perhaps it held more sentimental value.'

'Yes, I expect that's it,' Nat said. 'So, this record brings it full circle. It ties Jessie Chilcott back to Jessie Bates.'

'Yes, it does,' Tayte said. Through the genealogical records they had now seen, they knew without doubt that Jessie Bates became Jessie Black, who through marriage became Jessie Chilcott, who through her last will and testament had provided an irrefutable connection back to her original Bates name.

Nat's brow began to furrow. 'But how did she find them all – her brother and her sisters, I mean?'

'Maybe you're overlooking something.'

'I am?'

Tayte nodded, smiling warmly. 'Perhaps Jess never lost them.'

ACKNOWLEDGEMENTS

My thanks to Jenni Davis and Sandra Mangan for editing this book, to Kath Middleton for proofreading it, and to my wife, Karen, for her untiring support and contribution to all my books.

A special thank you to you for reading this book. I hope you enjoyed it. If you did, please tell someone. If you can find the time, please consider rating or reviewing it. Your support is very much appreciated.

ABOUT THE AUTHOR

Photograph © Karen Robinson

Steve Robinson is a London-based crime writer. He was sixteen when his first magazine article was published and he's been writing ever since. A keen interest in family history inspired his first million-copy bestselling series, the Jefferson Tayte Genealogical Mysteries, and with *The Penmaker's Wife* and *The Secret Wife* he is now expanding his writing to historical crime, another area he is passionate about.

The idea for his Jefferson Tayte series came to him in 2007, on his return from a trip to Cornwall, where the first book is set. In the five years that followed, he wrote the first three books in the series, all the while trying to find a publisher for them. In 2012 he published the books via Kindle Direct Publishing, and following their success, eighteen months later he signed a four-book deal with Amazon Publishing. The books were released in March

2014 under the Thomas & Mercer mystery and thriller imprint, and since then a further three books in the series have been published, taking the total to seven. In December 2019 his first non-Jefferson Tayte book, *The Penmaker's Wife*, was released. It was chosen as an 'Editor's Choice' book, and was nominated for the 2020 Crime Writer's Association Historical Dagger award, and the 2020 Costa Coffee book award in the 'Best Novel' category. Steve can be contacted via his website, www.steverobinson.me, or his Facebook page, www.facebook.com/SteveRobinsonAuthor, where you can also keep up to date with his latest news.

Printed in Great Britain
by Amazon